ALBANUS

Soldier To Martyr

For Heather

ALBANUS

Soldier To Martyr

JOHN AUBIN

© John Aubin 2025

Published by John Aubin Books

All rights reserved. No part of this book may be reproduced, adapted, stored in a retrieval system or transmitted by any means, electronic, mechanical, photocopying, or otherwise without the prior written permission of the author.

The rights of John Aubin to be identified as the author of this work have been asserted in accordance with the Copyright, Designs and Patents Act 1988.

A CIP catalogue record for this book is available from the British Library.

ISBN 978-1-7396959-6-5 (Paperback)
ISBN 978-1-7396959-7-2 (ePub)

Typeset by Clare Brayshaw

Manufacturer: York Publishing Services Ltd
64 Hallfield Road, Layerthorpe, York YO31 7ZQ
Tel: 01904 431213 | Email: enquiries@yps-publishing.co.uk
Website: www.yps-publishing.co.uk

Represented by: Authorised Rep Compliance Ltd.
Ground Floor, 71 Lower Baggot Street, Dublin D02 P593, Ireland
www.arccompliance.com

CONTENTS

	Pages
THE ROAD: Out of Battle	10-41
THE CITY: Awakening	42-93
THE ARENA: Conversion and Sacrifice	94-185
THE HILL: Execution	186-189
SYNCHRONICITY OF LIGHT: AD305 – the present	190-191
AFTERWORD	192-193

THE ROAD

Out of Battle

1

Sudden terror in the town, bodies flattened on the ground, children screaming, dogs racing about, barking, howling.

He watched the enemy come closer in their armoured carriers, and, standing up above the wall, loosed a magazine into one of the crawling steel flanks, causing the helmeted head in the turret to fall down out of sight. Others of the militia were firing too, until a shell found their position, spreading flesh and splintered bone high and wide in a burning cloud. He fired again into the chaos, then, his ammunition spent, fell back behind the wall, awaiting the end.

It did not come. The carriers with their rattling, squealing tracks continued on, firing as they passed. No foot soldiers were following up. Some people were struggling to their feet. Others lay still. A child's head, like that of a doll, rolled in the gutter. A dog was sniffing at it. A shot rang out, and the dog ran off, dragging a rear leg.

'Missed the brute!'

He was a tall man of middle years, dark-skinned with black hair and a thick beard. He wore a black cassock, the skirts hitched up to show knee-length breeches, socks and boots. A black cap with a high crown sat squarely on his head. A wooden crucifix hung at his chest, swaying as he moved. About his shoulders, falling to his waist, was a cape of dark leather, inset with silver studs, a hood attached, now pulled back to his shoulders.

'Who are you?' demanded the soldier, pointing his rifle at him, although he had nothing left to fire. The man still held his pistol. The soldier trusted no one.

'I am a priest. Here, you have this.' He handed the soldier the pistol. 'I found it on the ground. I've never fired one before.' He indicated the headless child. 'But this is beyond obscenity.'

A woman, spying the small body, began shrieking. She collapsed, covering it with her own, sobbing convulsively. The priest lifted her up by the shoulders and wrapped her in his arms. She quietened, and fell on her knees before him, her anguished face raised to his, streaming with tears. She had fair hair and skin.

'The child is with God now,' the priest said. His voice was deep and assured.

The soldier turned away. He did not believe in any god. He walked over to where his men had fought, but could find nothing but a smoking crater and scattered body parts. He doubled over, retching. He had fought beside those men for many months. Now he was the only one alive.

Spilt ammunition was strewn about a broken machine-gun. He collected as many of the shining rounds as he could find, reloaded his automatic rifle, and put the rest in the pouches strapped to his olive-green camouflage uniform. He unslung the pack he carried on his back and pushed the pistol into it. He was bare-headed, his helmet lost in the fight, showing a blond crop of short, wiry hair. He looked for his helmet amongst the scorched debris on the ground, but could not see it. He did not know what to do. His militia unit had made its last stand. Now he was on his own.

He had to get out of this town. Perhaps he could find others in the countryside who were continuing the fight. Perhaps, though, he had had enough: he would head home.

Home was the City in the river valley beyond the distant hills to the north. He had heard the enemy had occupied all of that region and made the City their capital. They had killed his mother and his brothers. That was when he had left to fight. It had been seven years ago – long years when all he had known was fighting, moving on, and fighting once more, over and over again. He had been good at it and he had been lucky – very lucky. But he was defeated at last. He knew that now for sure.

So perhaps he should accept the amnesty that they held out to all those who still resisted them. But what then would he do? He had no trade, no skills, other than killing. Yet, it might be best to return home where some might still remember him. They could help him to find work.

He was determined to live for himself now, not to die for someone else's cause, however noble it had once seemed.

2

As the soldier walked from the town, passing the last outlying houses, many wrecked by blast, the road lined with burnt-out vehicles and heaps of smoking rubble, there were scornful cries behind him: "Ad enough, 'ave yer, soldier boy?'.... 'Shame on yer, ye've brought us more harm than any good ye've done'....'Now, get the f--- out and find some other place to fight.'

He walked on for an hour or so, wary of another enemy patrol, watching the sky carefully for the hovering eyes of drones. He was not so worried about war planes. He knew most of the very few still airborne were engaged far to the east where some heavy fighting still continued – or so he had been told some weeks back. There was now a sense abroad that it would soon all be over and the enemy State would have won.

He tensed at the sudden sound of steps behind him, and moved at once to the shelter of the trees at the side of the road, unslinging his rifle. He was wary of roadside bombs, many planted years back by the local militia, but the ground looked safe enough – a grassy, tree-lined bank, beyond which lay open fields where a few thin cattle pulled miserably at the scrub-covered ground.

Peering out from the trees, he saw a black-clothed figure on the road nearly upon him, a bundle on a pole over his shoulder, his black hat crowning his head. The soldier had raised his rifle, but lowered it when he realised it was the priest.

'Ah, I'm glad I have caught up with you,' said he, approaching out of breath. 'I saw you leave and I followed as soon as I had given some small help back there.'

'That town is not where you live then?'

'No, I was passing through when the soldiers came suddenly. I did not think there would be fighting.'

'We had made a stand there. We were tired of running.'

'A futile gesture, I have to say. Many died needlessly because of it.'

'That is what happens in war, sir priest. But I have no wish to be condemned by you. So how may I help you now?'

'I thought we might travel together, as we seem to be going in the same direction. Two are safer on the road than one, most likely.'

'Because I am a soldier and will keep you safe? So we do have our uses then.'

'No, because you are a fellow human being and I seek companionship. I know that you are a brave man and your cause is a good one.'

'Where are you heading?' asked the soldier.

'I don't know for sure. But to the north, very likely.'

'It is from there that the enemy rule most of our land now.'

'I know.'

'What is your purpose then, priest?'

'Why, to convert them to the true God. To Christ, who is the bringer of peace.' The priest sounded almost surprised at the question. 'I am a follower of Christ with a mission to spread his word.'

'They will not listen to you. They have already condemned your god. I too have heard of a Christ, one who is called Jesu, if I recall rightly. You will not be allowed to worship him under the new rule.'

'Then we shall do so in secret, until the truth is known and we are stronger.' The priest stood up straight, his head erect, his dark face lit by a sudden ray of sunlight piercing the grey clouds.

The soldier fixed him with his gaze, his eyes hardened by the many years of suffering he had endured. 'They will kill you and all your followers.'

'Then they must do so. Yet others will rise up, for Christ will not be denied. In time, he shall live here again to destroy the evil in men's hearts that the devil has allowed.'

'Ah, you talk of devils now. That is something I *can* believe in. I have seen many of them these past years.'

'Then you too can believe in God,' said the priest eagerly, clutching at the soldier's arm. 'If you know there is a devil, why can you not believe in God too?'

'Because men grow into devils and I have seen their work all about me, but I have seen little of a god, any god, let alone a loving one, as I know yours to be.'

'Oh, that is good – very good. So then the true God is not entirely unknown to you.'

'I had my schooling,' the soldier said, sounding a touch offended. 'Yes, I knew of him once. Some with me in the war kept him beside them; or tried to do so. They would pray to him in their earth holes as the mortar bombs fell upon them. They would pray when the flights of rockets screamed overhead. They would pray before our attacks, when we went against them with bayonets to kill them hand to hand. Yet it did them little good. They died just the same. You see, sir priest, there is no room for gods on a battlefield with the killing going on, the flesh and bone split open, the entrails dripping in the trees, the brains oozing out of broken skulls.'

'I disagree,' the priest said sharply. He looked into the soldier's face. 'That is where you will find God first and foremost.'

'So why does he not stop it?!' cried the soldier, impatient of this nonsense now, eager to be on the move again. Looking back up the road, he was instantly alert.

'Quick!' The priest had begun a reply, but the soldier grabbed hold of him and pulled him from the road bank through the trees into the adjacent field. A thick clump of bushes grew there, and the soldier pushed the priest in amongst them, flat on his face in the long grass, then joined him there, his rifle with its curving magazine thrust out in front of him.

'Something's coming,' he whispered. 'Perhaps another patrol. I saw the sun flash on a windscreen. Keep out of sight and they will go past.'

But they did not. The roar of an engine came closer and closer, and then, with a squeal of brakes, it shut off, close to them. There was an interchange of voices. The soldier tensed, prone on the ground, pulling his rifle in nearer to him, his hand on the trigger.

They heard footsteps thrashing through the grass, stopping somewhere very near. The soldier could see a pair of good leather boots, and, falling onto them now, rolls of greenish cloth – trouser legs. Someone was squatting down to relieve himself. The hiss of piss streaming into the grass. Why did he not see them? Then suddenly, a shrill cry of alarm and the feet began to jerk away.

The soldier rose to his feet, firing in the same movement as he fixed his target. The enemy was not a man but a pretty-faced girl, struggling to pull up her trousers, her helmet lying at her feet and her chestnut-coloured hair bundled up and clipped behind.

He hit her with two short bursts in the chest. She was knocked backwards against a bush as if by a gigantic punch, her arms spread wide, her body slithering slowly to the ground. She lay still. He had killed her. He had not wished to kill a woman. But there had been no choice. Her companions would have heard the shots and now be coming for him. The priest was already at the side of the dead girl and speaking a mumbo-jumbo of words over her.

'Keep down, priest!' the soldier shouted. He had spotted one of the enemy – male, this time – rounding the front of the truck parked at the roadside, a machine pistol in his hands. The soldier fell to the ground, rolling over, once twice, three times, causing the enemy's fire to pass over his head. Then, sighting his rifle instantly, he pumped three shots into the man's neck and head, which exploded in a spray of blood and brains, the blood continuing to jet from the fallen body.

Firing bursts into the cab and through its canvas sides, the soldier ran to the rear of the lorry, ripping apart the ties holding the canvas opening together. He fired a further burst into the interior, then peered cautiously within. There was nothing living or dead there, only a heap of cardboard boxes, several of which had been torn open by bullets, their contents scattered.

Reaching inside, the soldier picked up a teddy bear, its brown, furry stomach leaking a stuffing of plastic chips, a doll beside it with a black flouncy skirt, one leg half-ripped off.

'Toys. Bloody toys,' he muttered. He searched further. 'More bloody toys. No weapons, no clothing, no food, no water: nothing of any f---ing use!'

The lorry was of no use either. To travel in it, assuming the engine still worked after all the firing, would only invite the enemy's attention. Its absence on whatever strange mission it had been bound would soon be noticed.

Seeing the priest was now speaking over the bloodied body by the road, he called out. 'Let's get away – now! Over the fields. The road will be full of them soon when they find out what's happened.'

The soldier set a course across a broad field, devoid of cover. They were in the open here, but on the ridge ahead there was a wood that would provide shelter from view. There, he could pause and make a new plan. Glancing behind him, he saw the priest was following only slowly, his pole with its burden over his shoulder. His black-clad figure, with the silver studded cape and the round high hat, looked exceptionally exposed amongst the low scrub and tussocks of grass, like a giant beetle crossing a green-coloured plate. The sooner they were beneath the trees, the better. He called out for him to hurry up.

As the soldier climbed higher towards the ridge, he was able to see more of the road below. Thankfully, it remained clear of traffic as far as he could make out to north and south. But they would come! They would come! He knew that. They would want those toys! He chuckled at the thought. Had the toys been meant for some children's party, hoping to win over the minds and souls of the people? It was not like this enemy to worry about such trivial matters.

At last among the trees, he sat down on the stump of a tree – from the freshness of its surface only recently cut – his rifle planted between his knees, watching the priest still toiling towards him. His crucifix on its chain had become pushed to one side by his exertions, and was caught up with the hand holding the pole. He struggled the last few yards, breathing hard, to where the soldier sat.

'Here, sir priest, rest awhile.' The soldier jumped up from the tree stump, while the priest thankfully took his place. After a time, when his breathing had recovered, the priest said abruptly: 'You did not have to kill those two.'

'I think I did! Or we would both be dead now.'

'There was no need to open fire.'

'And then they would have killed or captured us; and, for me at least, that would have meant death.'

'But, my son, why do you not try the path of peace?'

The soldier's patience, long held in, snapped. 'Look, you old fool, I don't share your faith or its ridiculous views. I've spent seven years as a soldier, day after day avoiding death by inches, and I aim to keep alive as long as I can. I don't need you with me. I didn't ask you to come with me. Why don't you f--- off and find someone else to plant your poison in?'

'And what's more,' he said into the silence that followed. 'I am not your son.'

'All are my sons and daughters,' the priest replied calmly. His bearded, dark face was serene, yet his eyes full of passion. 'For that is at the essence of my faith. As Christ is the son of God, so are we his sons and daughters too. I am ordained into these truths and thus I know I speak for him. It is my life, my purpose.'

'Even if it's not wanted?'

'Particularly so.'

The soldier turned his back and walked further into the woods before halting. He breathed in deeply. There was a musky smell on the air. Summer was coming to an end. He could see that the edges of the leaves were turning into yellows and browns. Soon the rains would arrive. He did not wish to be on the road in the rain and the cold. And then winter would follow. And the winters of this country, particularly in the hills ahead, could be severe, as he remembered from the frozen trenches in the eastern lands he had endured year after year. But there would be no braziers of burning coals to stand beside now. No food and drink brought up by supply lines through the frost and snow. No cheery chat and laughter with comrades, who might be here one day, then gone the next, to be replaced by others. Now he was on his own.

And, if he were honest with himself, he had to confess he did not really know what his purpose was now. What had he survived these long years for? At the end, to surrender all that he had ever fought for? To take the easy path of acceptance which the priest seemed to be suggesting? How simple that might be for an ordinary citizen. But as a soldier, he felt he would have to give up his very being to surrender himself to these new rulers who had once been his enemy. Would such a surrender not be seen to be down to his exhaustion, his weakness, his cowardice even? It was a difficult dilemma, for which there seemed no immediate solution. Yet how much he wanted now to be at peace!

He turned back to the priest, who was still seated on the tree stump: 'I am sorry, sir. I spoke to you intemperately. I spoke in a way I did not really mean. You have your calling and I have mine. I will respect yours. I do not blame you for condemning mine. I hate it as much as you do. Yet, it has been necessary. I believe I have saved more lives than I have taken.'

The priest rose and took his hand. 'You are a man of much courage and determination. I saw those qualities in you when we first met. Let us stay together, and perhaps you will allow me to tell you more of the God I follow and his son Jesus Christ.

'Perhaps,' said the soldier, impressed by the earnestness of the priest's words, although he believed the latter's hopes of him were doomed to failure. 'Let us take one pace at a time, for I am uncertain of my future at present.'

'One pace at a time then,' repeated the priest with a smile.

'Yes, for if I am truthful with you, sir priest, I have somewhat lost my way. I need to have a plan for whatever future there might be for me.'

He added hastily, seeing the priest's eyes resume their earnest, devotional look: 'By that I mean a literal, factual plan, not one about my soul and god's purpose for me, and all that sort of airy-fairy stuff. Now is not the time for that, sir, intending you no disrespect. I – we, for I do accept your companionship – must keep off the main roads for a while and take to the back lanes, passing through out-of-the-way places only, hoping to find houses to take us in and give us food and shelter, until we can reach the City, which I am headed for. Then, I will have to think further, for in the City the enemy now rule the new State through their Party, which soon will come to control us all. It could be a dangerous place for anyone who has fought them and not surrendered to them. My father's house where I was raised will probably be in other hands now.'

'The way to the Lord's house is always open,' said the priest.

Those words did not help the soldier. Yet, it seemed strange to him that they did not annoy him now either, and even brought him some vague sense of comfort, though he soon dismissed such an absurd idea from his mind.

'I do not know your name,' said the priest.

Of course, the soldier thought, if we are to travel together, we need to know each other better, yet to call him priest seems correct to me. Behind a soldier there is a man with a name, but behind a priest, who knows? Was not a priest born to be such, and priest the only name he has?

'My birth name is Albanus,' he answered. 'That is in the old Latin language, I have been told. My surname is Detrichen. My father was a professor at the university in the City. He taught of the ancient Greeks and Romans, and he wrote books about their history. He opposed the Party's revolution – indeed was outspoken in opposition to them – and he was fortunate to escape them when one morning they came for him as he lectured. So while searching for him at our house, they murdered my mother and my two brothers instead. Whether my father still lives, I know not, yet it is likely he is dead. I was at college that terrible day, and so escaped them. I ran away to fight. That was at the very beginning of the war. I have been a soldier ever since. You might just call me soldier, but Albanus, I will not mind. And your name, sir?'

'By the same token, you should call me priest, as most do. My name, however, is Amphibalus – but that is because of the cape I wear, which belonged to the Abbot who taught me. It was once much longer, a cloak indeed of some value, which later was cut short and decorated, as you see it now. I was an orphan, you should know, with no name yet given me. The good Abbot presented me with the cape, which covered me from head to foot, I being but a boy then. The sight made him laugh – and he laughed little. He thus thought that the Latin word for cloak would suit me. We used Latin much of the time, you understand.'

'It is strange then, priest, how we are connected through the ancients.'

'The ways of God are not strange, my son, although they may seem so at times, for he has a purpose for us all, as we shall surely discover.'

3

As the sun began to sink, declining to a reddish greyness in the western sky, they came by a narrow lane lined with thick hedgerows to a farm house of considerable age, judging by the great stones in its white-washed walls and its covering of deep, untrimmed thatch, thick with moss above the central door and the large, mullioned windows. They had walked for many hours, and seen no one but a labourer or two working in the fields, and, on one occasion, closer by, a woman and children beside a smoking bonfire, who looked at them curiously as they passed. The priest hailed them, raising his hat, but there was no answer, although a dog was loosed into the lane and ran for a while barking at their heels. They had had little to eat – just a piece of cheese taken from the priest's bundle and an unripe apple or two from a tree by the lane, washed down with water from a stream that the soldier judged pure enough.

'I know this place,' said the priest, greatly surprising the soldier.

'How is that? Do you know this part of the country then? You have not said so.'

'There are a great number of things I have not told you, my son. Your assumptions are not my fault.'

'No, of course, not.' The soldier unslung his rifle from his shoulder and, placing its butt against a bank, stood leaning upon it. He was weary and very hungry. He sought no argument now.

'I have been here preaching,' the priest told him. 'Before the war when Christianity was common amongst the people; let's see, perhaps seven years ago. I had quite a congregation then, I recall. I wonder if the same family is still present.'

They were, it seemed, for to the soldier's astonishment a beautiful young woman with long tresses of blonde hair came at a stumbling run from out the door of the house. She wore the traditional local costume of embroidered blouse with short, puffed sleeves and long black skirt, brocaded in patterns of white and red. Draped across her shoulders was a tawny-coloured cardigan, its arms dangling down.

'It is priest Amphibalus, is it not? I am not wrong, am I? Of course, I am not. I remember you so well – that cape of yours, your bearded face – although I was then but a child. Oh, father, how pleased I am to see you. This terrible war....'

And suddenly, to the soldier's surprise, she was crying and falling on her knees at the priest's feet; tears of pain or tears of joy, the soldier could not judge, perhaps a mixture of both.

The priest raised her to her feet. 'Why, Janita. How you have grown! And your father and mother. Are they...?'

The woman's tears came again. 'My mother lives: she is growing very frail. There she is now.'

The soldier followed her outflung arm and saw an old lady framed in the doorway, her black-clad body supported by a stick.

'But my father...' the tears turned to sobs '...he was killed nearly two years ago. They had shelled our village for no reason at all. He had gone there with the cart to fetch some supplies, and was hit. We were told there was no body to bury.'

More tears came as she continued to cling to the priest, her face contorted and gasping against the black cloth of his cassock.

Eventually, guided by the priest, she pulled herself up straight, apologising for what she called her weakness. She looked with some anxiety at the soldier as he stood a distance away, her eyes on his rifle. The priest now introduced him, and, as was still the custom amongst country people, she made a small curtsy to him while he bowed his head. He noted that she limped badly; one leg seemed to be shorter than the other.

The priest and he then greeted the old lady at the door with similar formality, and they went inside. The heavy door slammed to. For the first time in many days the soldier found himself shut off from the world outside. It was a feeling which was comforting yet disturbing at the same time – the latter because he was no longer in control of where he was and had no way of seeing what might come upon him next.

The soldier sat in a large, high-ceilinged room, with a wide central window that looked out over gardens towards fields beyond. A number of tall trees with broad, spreading crowns, the leaves already turning to autumn colours, stood to the right of the soldier's view. As he watched, a flight of black birds – rooks very likely – were settling to their evening roost. He raised to his lips the beaker of pale yellow wine he had been given, and drank thirstily.

The room was furnished with heavy old furniture, carved and panelled in dark wood – a dresser lined with blue and white plates, and a sideboard whose thick doors looked like they could stop the charge of a bull. They were topped by a line of books in golden bindings, stacked against the roaring heads of two cast-iron lions. The heavy chairs and sofa were evidently made more for appearance than for comfort.

From the depths of the armchair he had been ushered to, the soldier bent forward to peer at a man who had just entered the room. He was tall and powerfully built, with long brown hair falling to his shoulders, dressed in a leather jerkin and much patched, thick woollen trousers, the ends of which were stuffed into gaiters above stockinged, and now bootless, feet. He moved soundlessly into the room, then stood at its centre looking around him. His eyes passed swiftly over the old lady and Janita and fastened onto the soldier, and in particular on the rifle which he had insisted on keeping beside him: it was propped against his chair, its barrel within easy reach of his right hand.

'What is happening here?' he asked in a thick growl of a voice. 'Who is this man?' – and then before anyone could answer, to the soldier's further surprise, his eyes alighted on the priest, and he at once went to kneel before him, seeking his hand that he might kiss it. 'Father. I thought we should never see you again. This is a miracle truly.'

'No, my son. The miracle is in God's love for us, as always and ever will be. The fault is mine, for I have neglected all of you here. It is why I return now.'

Surely that is not true, thought the soldier. The priest is only here because I decided to come this way, and he has accompanied me. Yet, although that reality was clear to him, he nonetheless felt a strange uncertainty. The priest emanated a power and a mystery he could not explain. Perhaps, indeed, it was he – the soldier – who had been following the priest. He was momentarily puzzled, and it was not often he had allowed himself such an uncertainty in recent years. Uncertainty meant confusion. And confusion could bring sudden death.

'This is my brother,' said Janita, looking across at the soldier. 'His name is Venrig. Venrig, please give greeting to er, er....' she realised she had no name for the soldier '...this soldier who has brought Father Amphibalus to safety here out of the fighting.'

'My name is Albanus.' The soldier rose and waited for Venrig to clamber to his feet before taking his hand. His grip was hard, the skin rough and calloused.

'Welcome to this house, Albanus,' he said. 'Your name is unusual. From where do you come?'

'From the City in the northern province,' he answered. He then told the story of his name, as he had recently given it to the priest, adding: 'It means 'of the fair' in Latin. My brothers were older than me and dark-haired, you see. I was the only one whose hair was light.'

He thought: I do not know this man. What I have told him is enough for now.

'When did you meet Father Amphibalus?'

'Just this morning.' He would say no more. If the priest wished to add further details, he could not stop him, but the priest was silent.

'Are you a Christian?'

The sudden question surprised the soldier into an answer. 'You mean, am I of the priest's religion? Do I follow his Christ? No, I do not. Gods are of little practical use in soldiering, and that's been my business much of my life.'

'God helps you in times of pain and danger. God sustains you in death.'

'I have survived until now without any god. I do not plan to die – not yet, anyhow.'

'It is best to be ready for death.'

The soldier was growing irritated by this conversation, which he had not sought and which he was coming to view as over-intrusive. Despite his need for food, should he not then leave now to make his own way beyond these walls? If the priest did not wish to come with him, then so be it. Safety, he considered, lay in maintaining his independence. It was how he had survived so far – that and the comradeship of the others who had shared his resolution, soldiered well, and did not talk of gods. Now they were dead – all of them – and he was alone once more. He rose from his chair and picked up his rifle.

'Where are you going?' It was Janita who spoke. She was quickly on her feet, staggering on her lame leg as she put her body between him and the door.

'I thank you all for your hospitality, but I must be on my way.'

'And where will you sleep tonight? From where will you get food?' Janita asked.

'Sit down,' said the priest. 'You insult our hosts.'

'If that is true, I regret it. But I did not ask to come here and I did not ask to be questioned on my beliefs and my purpose. I thank you all for your hospitality, but I shall go now.'

Janita stood determinedly against the door. He could not use physical force to move her. That would be unthinkable. He knew his position was growing ridiculous. Instead, he adopted a mocking attitude: 'It seems like your god wishes me to stay.'

'Oh, he does, most certainly,' the priest said, on his feet now also, taking the soldier by the arm and leading him back to his chair. The soldier knew he could not struggle either against the priest.

It was the old lady who spoke next to break the awkwardness, her voice high and bird-like and in a dialect the soldier found hard to follow. But he could just about understand that she was inviting everyone to share the meal that she had been preparing. This must be a custom of this house, he thought, for her son and daughter, the priest too, answered formally, bowing their heads in thanks while placing the palms of their hands together.

Perhaps this is a practice amongst Christians, the soldier considered. Is it then a danger to me, rather than a strength, that I am now amongst those whom I know the enemy little tolerates? Might they not come here to root out these people? After all, we are only some fifteen miles from the town where we fought them this morning. They might well have patrols out scouring the district. Yet, I think it safe enough to spend a night here and have the meal these people offer, for where else would I obtain food so late in the day, and in truth I am famished. There may be a risk in being here, but possibly a greater risk outside. I shall sleep, however, with my rifle close beside me.

The soldier and the priest, in fact, were to spend three nights at the house. Janita had fetched some clean clothes for the soldier the first night, taking away his camouflage trousers and jacket, shirt, underpants and vest to wash while he slept, and replacing them with others she told him had been her father's. They fitted him, although the trousers were a little short in the leg.

The soldier made no protest. Before the sudden enemy breakthrough, he had been for weeks in the front-line trenches. The sense of vulnerability that losing his uniform caused him, if only temporarily, was outweighed by the prospect of having it returned cleaned and pressed. Venrig also lent him some washing things and a razor with which he was able to scrape away much of the stubble he had grown in the last few days.

On the second evening, after a day in which the soldier had helped Venrig with tasks about the farm, always keeping his rifle close to hand, it was to his great alarm – for he was worried that news of his presence here with the priest might reach the ears of someone in contact with the enemy – that, after taking a walk at a distance from the farm, he returned to find a host of people, of whom he had been told nothing, gathering together in the main yard. They were all country people, families, men with their wives and children, single men and women too, even a few babes in arms. They had come – and were still coming – along the lane, by bicycle or on foot, a number too across the open fields, one at least astride a plodding horse.

He re-entered the house and found the priest, who was just about to go outside. The priest told him, reassuringly, 'Albanus, my friend, they are of my former congregation here: they have learnt of my return and wish me to bless them and give thanks to God for keeping them safe in these troubled days. Do not worry. They will not betray us. There will be no Judas amongst them.'

The people assembled in the great barn that stood at one side of the yard, some standing, others seating themselves on the crates and drums that had been set out on the stone-paved floor. It was a large, wooden-sided barn with a high roof crossed by great timbers. At the far end was a low platform, on which the priest stood in his black cassock, wearing his high-crowned hat. On a broad plank laid across two barrels, he had placed the wooden crucifix he normally wore about his neck with its carved image in white of the dying Jesu hung upon the cross. Beside it was a silver chalice that he had brought out from the bundle he had carried here. Janita was even now filling it with red wine, fetched from her mother's kitchen. Beside the chalice she had placed two long loafs of bread.

The soldier, wearing now his freshly-washed combat clothes, the various straps and pouches of his harness re-attached, did not appear to be a concern to the gathered people, although he had received some curious looks at first. He stood alone at the rear of the barn, close to the door. His rifle he had placed out of sight in a wooden bin beside him, not wishing to alarm anyone on an occasion that he recognised, despite his own scepticism, was to be one of their faith, and of peace.

A little girl wandered up to him and clutched his sleeve with her tiny hand. 'Dadda,' she said, making him smile and the people around to laugh.

The priest began the service by striking the bell which the soldier had seen Janita bring out from the house. Everyone joined in with the words that he began to intone – a prayer in Latin, it seemed: the soldier even recognised some of the words, in particular *pater noster*, repeated regularly. As he spoke, the priest spread his arms wide, his palms facing outwards. He makes the shape of their cross, the soldier thought. Many of the congregation were doing the same. One or two, including Janita, had fallen to their knees, their arms thrust out before them. Her mother stood, bent forward in the front row, with Venrig's strong arm about her.

And then the priest's words came in their own language: 'Our glorious Lord, bless your people who have gathered here to worship you, to confess their sins and to renew their faith in you, by taking your flesh as theirs, by drinking your blood, as you taught us, yes even as you were nailed to the cross to die for us.'

The priest then broke the bread and gave it to the people who came forward one by one to take it in their mouths, then to drink from the chalice, the bell being rung repeatedly as they did so by a small man in an old fashioned, black frock coat, who was assisting the priest.

Eventually, all had eaten a piece of the bread and drunk the wine, the children also, even the babes clasped by their mothers, the chalice being touched by the priest to their lips. All, that was, except the soldier, who had made no attempt to go forward, regarding the whole performance with a sardonic amusement, yet – he had to admit – with a measure of respect also. If this was what the people needed to help them survive these difficult times, then who was he to think it was anything other than good? The enemy had increasingly set itself against religion of any sort, yet he could not understand why, unless they thought the superstition undermined the practical good sense and obedience the new State demanded.

The people, including Venrig and his mother, she at a slow step clinging to his arm, were leaving the barn now. All were chattering happily amongst themselves, thanking the priest when they could get close to him. Some even shook the soldier's hand, perhaps thinking he had been posted there to protect them. It was hard to know. He smiled back at them in that hard way he had learnt on the battlefield, unwilling to say anything at all.

Indeed, if he had been asked, he would not have known why he had attended the service: the priest had not asked him to do so. Perhaps it was because already he felt a sense of companionship with the priest, who had told him again only this morning how much he wished to journey on with him. The soldier could not understand why. He would only very likely take him into further dangers. Why should the priest want this when it was clear now he could stay on here and be a comfort to these country people, at a time when all was changing about them?

And now here was the priest himself before him, his clear, black eyes in the dark face looking into his, his untrimmed beard seeming bushier than ever, so he had something of the look of a wild man – a man most fervent for his god.

'Albanus,' he said. 'Did you find meaning in our worship? Might you wish to join us on the path to Christ?'

This priest does not spare me his interest, the soldier thought, a little irritated. Why cannot he just accept what I have already told him?

'No, sir priest," he answered. 'I do not feel any such need. I would not fill my head with your beliefs or take part in your rituals. As I have told you, I have learnt to depend on my own wits. I cannot entrust myself to anything else on this earth, let alone beyond it.'

'One day, my son, you will have that need, and then you will understand. In the meantime, while we travel on together, I shall teach you.'

The soldier was exasperated. 'Why do you think that is necessary? Why do you wish to remain with me, anyhow?'

'Because, my son, that is what God tells me. And I am but his poor servant, so must obey him.'

The soldier said: 'If I am honest, I would not scorn your company, but I do not require your teaching.'

'Well,' the priest said gravely, his voice raised so he could be heard over the babble of conversation of the last of those who were leaving the barn and calling out their farewells. 'That is a start, anyhow.' He gave a deep rumble of laughter. 'We shall be pilgrims together following the same path.'

'But to where, sir priest? I seek a home again. For what do you journey?'

'I am travelling in the Lord's work, my son. Towards the heaven that awaits those who follow him. It is what all must desire – to know God's truth.'

The soldier sighed. He bent to remove his rifle from the bin where he had placed it. The barn was empty now, except for Janita, whom he could see still standing by the makeshift altar from which the priest had conducted the service. It was growing dark, the evening now well-advanced. Janita had lit a candle, which she was holding out before her. The flame flickered, sending shadows chasing about the barn. The crucifix stood to one side of her, the white crucified figure upon it seeming to move in the flickering light, as if it would come down from the cross, and move towards them, the body made whole again. This illusion did not alarm the soldier. Instead, he had the sudden, strange feeling that he would welcome it.

He came up to Janita, his rifle balanced barrel-downwards in one hand, and took the candle from her into the other. 'Can you see? Don't stumble. The light is going very quickly.' He blew out the candle, setting it down, and then took her hand in his, helping her in her limping walk to the doorway of the barn. The priest had now left.

'You are very beautiful,' he told her. The words came from nowhere. He had not intended to say them. He leant forward and gently brushed his lips against her cheek.

As she looked up at him, he saw there were tears filling her eyes, normally so brightly blue, and he did not understand. She did not speak.

It was now very dark. The host of people had all disappeared and they were alone. The soldier felt the air opening, fading, and closing all about him, as if something important was moving deep within him. He shrugged the feeling off and shouldered his rifle. The two walked to the house, their fingertips touching.

4

The next morning, the priest, his cape once more about his shoulders, his head topped by his black hat, told the soldier he was going to spend the day visiting the homes of his flock – as he termed his followers – in the surrounding area, some of whom had been unable to come to his service. He would go by himself, he said, and return in the evening. The next day, as they had both now agreed, they would leave and continue their journey.

So the soldier was left alone at the house. Venrig had not asked for his help this day, and had gone off somewhere on his own. After their breakfast, Janita was not to be seen either. He was disappointed by her absence: she had said little to him that morning.

The soldier, hoping that his presence at the farm would not by noised abroad by any of the worshippers yesterday, felt uneasy. He took up his rifle, stripped it down, taking out the curving magazine and unloading the rounds one by one, then cleaning and oiling it before reloading, checking the ammunition in his body pouches too. Only the old lady was in the house. He tried talking to her, but it was not easy to make out what she said in answer. He stood in the kitchen, trying to accustom himself to the quick rhythm of her speech, as she boiled a great kettle over an ancient stove. After a while, he managed to understand her somewhat better.

She made him tea, and he thanked her with a bow, taking the vast earthenware mug in both hands and watching her as she continued to work away at some small task or other, chattering at him in her high voice.

She was speaking of Venrig; what a good son he had turned out, although her husband, whose given name had been Hendreth, had once thought him lost to the town's drinking houses, or worse: she did not say what that 'worse' might have been, but the soldier could guess. Hendreth had been a good husband and a hard worker, she said, but he had a great temper and he had often shouted at his son for idling, and then one day Venrig had had enough and attacked him with his fists – his own father – and so Hendreth had thrown him out.

That had been shortly before the war, and they had learnt later Venrig had joined the militia and fought at the front too, but had returned after only a year, or so – a changed man, now much quieter and thoughtful. It was just as well, the old lady added, or otherwise Hendreth could not have continued to run the farm by himself, as there was no labour to hire, for all were at the war or in hiding. And then Hendreth had been killed. She told the story of this, how she had not even had a body to put under the ground, without any outward sign of emotion, rather surprising Albanus.

She showed much more feeling when she went on to speak of the priest. It was his influence, she said, which had persuaded Vendrig to return. She did not know exactly how that had happened, but she was sure it was he who had changed her son for the better and brought him home, during one of the enemy's periods of amnesty. Father Amphibalus has particular powers, she said, looking up at the soldier, a smile now lighting up the wrinkled berry of her face.

That is likely true, thought the soldier. I have already experienced a little of his power myself. And he thought of how the priest had attached himself to him out of nowhere, and walked with him, as if what they did was long written down and there was no other course for either of them to follow.

Later, in the drawing room where the soldier sat examining a volume of maps he had brought down from a shelf, the old lady moved about him, saying the occasional word, while she flapped with a duster at some of the surfaces that the soldier could see were thick with dust. He heard a door open and shut, and tensed, reaching out for his rifle that he kept beside him.

The old lady laughed. 'It's only Janita,' she said. 'She teaches some mornings at the school further down the lane. She usually returns about this time.'

Janita did not come into the room, however. Perhaps she had gone to rest in her bedroom, which he knew was across the corridor from the one that the priest and he shared. He very much wanted to see her. Why? He did not really know, perhaps just because she was a young woman who was soft and gentle and trusting after all the horrors of battle he had been through. These were the qualities he wished to have about him now above all, which Janita most definitely possessed; but, more than that and against all common sense, he found himself being increasingly drawn to her as an attractive, desirable woman. He had told her she was beautiful. Had that been a mistake? Had she been offended by his forwardness?

He remembered with sudden shock that he had recently killed a woman of much the same age as Janita. It hadn't been necessary. He admitted that now. If he only he had waited a second or two, and not reacted as if in a battle still, he would have realised she was no danger to him. Both those soldiers might then have lived with their cargo of children's toys. Yet now they were dead and people would be grieving for them.

He rose to his feet and strode to the window. He could see sunlight gleaming on the grassy fields that sretched away from the house empty of man and beast, or indeed of any cultivated crop, it seemed. Where was Venrig? He had helped him yesterday. Clearly, much work on this farm needed to be done each day. It couldn't be left for long. Yet was that any concern of his? He would be gone tomorrow, unlikely ever to return.

The old lady was now talking to him again, a finger raised to her lips as she spoke, as if to indicate she had a secret to tell – by her manner, perhaps a considerable secret. And a terrible secret, it did prove to be. Why had she felt the need to tell him? Perhaps just to explain her daughter's disability to him, as if indeed he wanted to know that. If he had any idea of staying on here longer, then he might have been interested – for he would certainly have wished to court her – but surely then Janita in the fullness of time would have told him herself.

He was set on his course now, to take up his life again in the City, where it had begun – the settled, ordered City that he remembered and might still survive despite its takeover by the enemy; but at least there should be a peace of sorts there now and some type of normality. He could not see himself continuing to stay on at this farm, in an area still liable to enemy patrols, where there would be little future for him as, say, a farm worker under Venrig's control. That would not be what he wanted at all, with or without Janita at his side. And she might well repel his advances, in any event!

The terrible thing the old lady told him about Janita was this –

Hendreth had grown jealous of his own daughter. Janita was her mother's most precious child, much more so than Venrig could ever be, but then he was a boy and took after his father. Janita was her own to cherish. To Hendreth it was as if his daughter was taking his wife away from him, when she should have been more caring, more attentive of him and his needs. After all, it was he who worked so hard to keep the farm going, to buy them everything they needed, to bring them the very food they put into their mouths. To see his wife cooing over Janita, and playing with her, when she should have been looking after him, when he was tired and hungry and irritable, had brought on one of his sudden great rages. He had been drinking too.

One awful night he had picked up Janita when she had been crying – she was then only just over two years old – and whirled her tiny body about his head, then released her so that she fell heavily to the stone floor. One of her little legs was broken in two places. It could not be set properly, and so she grew up with a bad limp. She had never told Janita how she had come by her deformity. 'It is just one of those things – that God has allowed you to be born in this way,' was all she had said when Janita had once asked.

But Janita had seemed to know, anyhow, her young brain perhaps scarred with an imprint of the violence used against her, if not any understanding of it. She was always very wary of her father, never coming to him as a daughter naturally would, although Hendreth had tried very hard to make up for that one dreadful thing he had done to her. But his wife had never forgiven him. Years later, after she had got over the first shock at hearing he had been killed, she had felt almost glad of the news.

'She is a lovely girl,' the old lady said. 'Full of pity for those injured by the war. She does what she can to help them. She loves the birds and the animals of the fields and woods, and hates to see any who suffer – the boars and the deer that we used to kill for their meat, but are seldom seen now.'

'The whole village took part in those hunts.' she added, her eyes shining, thinking back on the days before the war. 'Now there is very little fresh meat to be got anywhere.'

'But the men don't seem to want my Janita. She is still pure, untouched. It is because of her limp. They have been taught that lameness is a sign of the devil. Given her sweet nature, such an idea is cruel and stupid. When she was at school, they made fun of her. She would come home crying.'

The old lady's eyes flashed. 'There is much ignorance about, much cruelty, which even the priest could not dispel. And he has been away from us for a long time.'

The soldier thought again of the priest: how was it then that I thought I had led him here from violence to a place of safety, when in fact our journey – or at least the last part of it – must have been familiar to him? And yet he said nothing until we reached this place. He shook his head in puzzlement.

The old lady had now left the room. Everything here is very strange, the soldier thought. He felt anxious, unsettled. It is as well then we are to leave tomorrow. The priest had told the soldier that the two were to be pilgrims together seeking God's path. Was that not a little fanciful, even deranged? Had the priest's mind grown unbalanced? Was he to walk with a madman?

Yet, he knew such imaginings were wrong. The priest had a presence about him – a power, a certainty – which he could not explain. Why then did he not remain with these people he knew – and the wider community about – who clearly loved him and needed him? He could surely obtain a living here ministering to them. Why, instead, did he wish to accompany a stranger to the City where there would certainly be many dangers for him?

The priest had still not returned by the time it was growing dark, and nor had Venrig, as far as the soldier could tell. He had not seen Janita either, so perhaps she was still in her room. He had expected to find her in the kitchen helping her mother, but the old lady had disappeared somewhere into the bowels of the house.

He took up his rifle, slung it by its strap from his shoulder, and went outside, seeing how the fields were beginning to darken as the sun sank lower, now half hidden behind a row of great pine trees standing to the west.

And then suddenly, there was Janita coming out of a shed, clasping a large bowl of hens' eggs to her breast. It was a task she was clearly used to, her free hand placed over the eggs against the jolting of her lurching walk. She wore a long, blue-patterned skirt and a black, sleeveless jerkin over a white blouse. He thought she looked very lovely, and he felt a wave of sympathy for her from what her mother had told him. He hastened to help her, but she declined his offer with a rather impatient thrust of one arm.

'I can well manage, sir, thank you.'

Then, as if regretting this dismissal, she stopped, looking up at him quite boldly. 'We are to have omelettes this evening,'

The smile that accompanied this statement, he thought a little forced. She looked pale. Perhaps she was not well.

'That sounds good.' He tried to smile back, but knew his look was also strained. There was something unsaid between them that must be causing this awkwardness, something perhaps neither wished to admit to.

And then, much to his surprise, in a rush of words that tumbled out of her as if their coming was as much an astonishment to her as to him, 'I would talk to you, sir. In private. If you come to my room after our meal, I shall be there.'

He muttered, 'Of course, if you wish it', then held the door to the house open for her, and she passed inside without looking at him again.

He walked on pondering the matter, passing through the long, yellowing grasses where the open fields began. In the distance, he made out the figures of the priest and Venrig as they appeared suddenly on the darkening horizon. The priest's silhouette was clear in his distinctive shoulder cape and hat: he was seated astride a mule led by Venrig, the group etched sharply against the evening sky.

As they came closer, the priest hailed the soldier jovially, both arms raised from the mule's back, as if in a blessing. For a moment, the soldier thought he would fall, and hastened forward to help him.

'Such fortune,' the priest called out, 'that Venrig should find me, and with a mule too. For my return journey was more wearisome than I had thought and I had become a little lost. I should not have travelled so far, but my sheep are spread far and wide and my will to minister to them can outdo what is practical.'

After the priest had slid down from the mule, assisted by the soldier, Venrig led the animal away to the stables. Other than for a grunt of greeting, he had said nothing. The soldier wondered at this, for Venrig had been agreeable enough to him earlier. He had a premonition that all might not be right. Was Venrig's loyalty assured? It was as well then they were leaving early the next day. He must be on his guard more than ever, probably with little sleep this night.

Janita had cooked the omelettes, bearing them from the kitchen to the dining room two by two as she finished them. The old lady sat beaming at the head of the great mahogany table. She was given the first omelette, which she began to pick at using a silver fork. The second was given to the soldier, and then of the next two, the first to the priest, who passed it on to Venrig, telling him to eat now, for he wished to be served last.

'Eat, eat everyone,' he boomed in his deep voice, when at last all were served and Janita was back at the table. 'The Lord will not mind us thanking him afterwards, rather than before.'

Clearing his plate, the soldier turned to Janita, who was still eating. 'That was delicious. With cooking like that, you would go straight to a man's belly and make him very happy.'

And then, judging by the silence those words brought, he wished he had not spoken. Janita looked embarrassed and Venrig gave him a look that might be interpreted as one of disbelief, or was it suspicion?

The priest, however, broke the awkwardness by raising his pot of ale to Janita, with the words, 'Bless you, my child', which brought a smile from her. Venrig then refilled his pot from a giant pitcher, which took two hands to hold. When he offered to pour for the soldier, the latter declined. He knew he must keep a very clear head this night.

Venrig shrugged and turned away. He then drank deeply, and filled his pot again. The soldier noted that Janita give him a glance of disapproval, while Venrig avoided his sister's eyes.

After the meal was over and the priest had offered up thanks, Janita cleared the plates from the table. The soldier made to help her, but she waved him away. He could sense Venrig's eyes fixed on him, and he wondered why. They went into the lounge where the priest began to regale them with the story of his day's travels. 'Such a welcoming. Such joy I received. They are good people, my sheep here – the very first of God's kingdom.'

Will there be no end to this nonsense, the soldier thought? Sheep and kingdoms, indeed. People survive, people help each other. It is called humanity. There is no need for any god to intrude. He was on edge, his instincts for danger aroused. His rifle was propped close to him. He could reach it in a trice. But he still felt unsafe. He should never have stayed in this place so long. What had he been thinking of? The priest seemed to have cast a spell over him.

Janita came into the room, and sat a while, listening to the priest. She did not seem her usual happy self. She looked very tired. We are all tired, the soldier thought. Tired of war, tired of struggle, tired of uncertainty. Despite what I might think otherwise, if the priest's god could end these things for me, then I too would follow him. But perhaps I am growing deluded as well. Man only survives by keeping his wits sharp.

He glanced at the hard metal shape of the rifle beside him, with its wooden butt, its protruding magazine, and its pierced firing chamber of cold, black steel. And by keeping a good friend like this too. How many had he killed with this one? He had no idea. A good number, he thought, and he remembered again the woman he had shot last of all, and felt a sudden sickness.

Janita stood up. 'I shall not be long,' she said. The soldier saw her glance at him, and there was a meaning there, so he knew the time had come. He waited a short while. Venrig was in a lengthy conversation with the priest, and the old lady's hands were fidgeting with some needlework she held on her lap, but it was clear her eyesight was too poor to do much to it now. He watched her hands pulling aimlessly at the threads.

He stood up. He picked up his rifle. No one was looking at him, so he left the room quietly. They would probably think he had gone to relieve himself. Why should he feel guilty, anyhow? He had done nothing wrong, nor was he planning anything underhand. Yet, some sense or other was drumming in his ears. Something might be about to happen – for better or for worse, he knew not. He held the rifle forward, advancing down the passageway, not trusting the shadows cast by the one oil lamp that hung there on its bracket. He came to Janita's door. It was opened quickly to his knock and he slid his body inside, his rifle at the ready, his finger curled over the trigger just in case.

5

'Ah, so you *have* come!' Janita was standing in the centre of the room. She ignored the pointing rifle, which Albanus immediately lowered.

A narrow bed with a pale pink eiderdown stood against one wall. That was all the soldier saw at a first glance – a quick scan to ensure that no one else was present – for the truth was that he did not want to be here at all. He felt trapped, uncertain. These were not sensations an alert soldier wished to have. He noticed how Janita's breast was heaving and she sounded out of breath, so she must be very nervous. But what of?

'What is it you want? he asked, impatient now. 'I cannot be long, or else they will wonder where I am.'

She held her hands out before her, intertwining the fingers in a continuous motion, clearly ill at ease. 'I needed to see you in private to ask your opinion.'

'Could you not have spoken to me outdoors?'

'Venrig watches me all the time. And I had not made up my mind then.'

'And now?'

'Can I come away with you and the priest tomorrow?'

Albanus was astonished. 'How can you? That would mean leaving your mother, and she clearly needs you.'

'I know,' she wailed, and he could see the distress in her face. 'I have no life here, you see. Time comes and goes and all I am is a drudge for Venrig, and for mother too, although I love her so. I know I would be safe with you.'

'I could not let you come. And the priest, who accompanies me now, would surely not allow it either. Why have you not asked *him*?'

'Because I know his answer would be no. He would tell me to say my prayers and to look after my family, whereas I am sick of this life.'

'I can understand that,' he said, more gently now. He touched her cheek, and she quivered at his touch. He knew now what the problem was. It was not just the boredom of her life here and her responsibilities. It was him she wanted to be with, to stay with him and to share a future with him.

He felt the weight of this responsibility so suddenly thrust upon him, much as he would have liked to take her in his arms and love her. He saw only beauty in her, and there had been many years when he had been without beauty in any form.

'When you kissed me yesterday,' she said tremulously. 'I felt my body dissolve for you. I know that is a ridiculous thing to say, and I am ashamed.'

He did not know what to answer.

'You see there are few men here, and those there are ignore me because of my affliction.' She said this in a rush, as if pleading for his understanding of her forwardness.

'You have no affliction,' he said, determined to gain control of the situation. 'You seem to manage very well. You will soon forget me and find a good man one day. For, as I have told you, you are beautiful and the right man will surely come to you soon.'

'Oh, God help me,' she moaned.

He made up his mind. 'Do you have paper here and something to write with?'

'Yes, I believe so. What do you want them for?' She turned from him and pulled open a drawer in a cabinet, producing a torn scrap of paper and a thick stub of pencil. She gave them to him.

He wrote quickly, pressing the paper against a panel of the door, and then handed it to her, which she received with a trembling hand, scarcely daring to look down at it.

He said: 'This is the address where I used to live in the City. I am going there now, hoping to find my father still alive, but it will be a miracle if he is. I have not heard from him for over seven years. He may have been captured and killed by them years ago, and his house taken over or destroyed. The Party, as you know, control the City now, and they rule there in everything. But, if in time you find you can leave your mother, and you still remember me, then you can seek me there. I shall be very happy to see you, honoured indeed, my sweet maid.'

He pretended a bow, while she looked on, with hope in her face again. 'But I tell you, you will have soon forgotten.....'

The door crashed open and there was a great shout in his ears. 'Just as I thought! You bastard, so you seek to f--- my sister, do you?!'

Janita screamed. The soldier spun round, and caught Venrig's arm as he lashed down at his head with a heavy brass candlestick, deflecting the blow, then grasping Venrig's heavy, flailing body and flinging it across the floor against the bed. He leapt upon him there, kicking at his groin and stabbing with his fingers at his eyes, while he, yelling in pain and fury, struggled to regain his feet.

'Janita, the rifle!' Albanus yelled.

'I have it,' a deep voice called. The priest stood in the doorway. 'It is safe with me.'

The soldier did not need it. With a further quick succession of blows, the last one delivered to the head with the same candlestick used against him, he reduced Venrig to unconsciousness, his body collapsed backwards, half-on and half-off the bed, the pink eiderdown already reddened by his blood.

Janita was shrieking: 'You've killed him! You've killed him!' Now she was covering her brother's prostrate form with her own. She gulped out in a flood of tears: 'I did nothing. I did nothing. We were only talking, Surely I'm allowed to talk.' She fled from the room, knocking against her mother who stood in the hallway, shaking. The priest tried to stop her, but she struggled free. 'I must get him water,' she gasped.

The soldier looked at the priest. 'I had no choice,' he said.

He had used those words before, he remembered. His body ached. His right fist felt broken. He took his rifle from the silent priest, who made no resistance, and left the room.

Some minutes later, he reappeared, with his webbing harness strapped on and bearing his rifle. 'I'm leaving now,' he said. 'I knew it was a mistake to stay here.'

'Where do you go?' the priest asked.

'Somewhere, anywhere. I need to be a soldier again. I've been off my guard. This is what happens.'

Janita was tending her brother's bleeding head, sponging it with water. The soldier saw the eyes flickering open, so he knew he was still alive. Janita's face was away from him. He did not want to see it again. He wondered if she had set him a trap. He would probably never know. Yet it was a great pity. For just one moment he had weakened. He had had the briefest vision of something lovelier and far softer for himself than the bitter, harsh life he had endured for years and was likely to continue for many more, something desperately yearned for, although he would not admit to that. And it had nearly got him killed. Survival was all about learning. He would not let his guard down again.

He bowed stiffly to all of them, muttered an apology to the old lady who stood weeping by the front door, and went out into the night, carrying his rifle across his body, alert once more to every danger that might come to him.

THE CITY

Awakening

6

The office walls were a greyish yellow in colour, the ceiling of white plaster smudged with circular patches of dirt, as if someone had been bouncing a football up and down against it in some idle game of yesteryear. The long, rectangular floor space was set with steel desks of various shapes and sizes, some bearing bright computer screens, but most with old typewriters and other equipment like the offices of many years ago.

The staff who sat behind the desks all wore a uniform baggy-grey boiler suit, which was synonymous with the Party – the Party being that of the victorious enemy who had made the City their new capital. They had conquered all the land that was worth conquering, although a sporadic resistance in some backward areas still went on. The emphasis now was on rule and governance and bringing the country into compliance with the Party's doctrines. This was being carried out with an elephantine efficiency, slow and ponderous, but overwhelming in its relentlessness.

At one of the desks, half way along the room, beneath a long-unwashed window pane, sat Albanus, no longer a soldier, for he had done now with soldiering and accepted his former enemy as his employer. This decision – a surprising one for him to take, but he had come to feel he had no other option

– had been helped greatly by the general amnesty granted by the State President to all 'who had been coerced into fighting against the Party's armies', but who now renounced violence and wished to support the Party by working for it. That clemency did not extend to any remnants of the former resistance militias who yet fought on in a few outlying places: they were decreed terrorists, to be hunted down and killed on sight. Surrender for them was not an option.

Today, Albanus led a team of clerks, organising the forms they must receive and check, and the further forms that were required to be filled in and sent off to Section K289/3 on the lower floor. If a mistake was made, it would be he who would get the blame, not the team member who was the cause of it. Two mistakes by a team leader, he had heard, and then you were out. As he knew he had been fortunate to obtain this job and the one-roomed flat in the slab-like concrete block that went with it, he did not want to lose these things now. So he berated his team each day to make sure their attention was strictly on their work.

When he had first entered the City, after discarding his uniform, his equipment, the pistol the priest had given him and his long-trusted rifle – he had sold all these to a trader he found in the southern suburbs for a modest sum and a second-hand suit of plain clothes – it had been to find that the house where his family had once lived was now a construction site for further blocks of flats and offices, some already being built. In fact, the street plan of the old City he had known had been largely eradicated, and a new geometrical grid laid out. There was no one around now who might have known his family or who could tell him if his father had survived the earlier purges, unlikely as that was, for he had been a marked man from the beginning.

Albanus remembered, still as vividly as that day seven years ago, seeing the dead bodies of his brothers in the hallway, and his mother too, who had been taken outside into the garden to be raped and shot. He had no idea where they might have been buried. The dead had no place of burial now, cremation being the accepted Party method of bodily disposal. All the registers of births, marriages and deaths had been destroyed when the City was bombed at the start of the revolution, and there appeared to be no new registers of the names of the departed that might be consulted.

By sheer chance, he had escaped the killings, and got away, vowing the vengeance he had now fulfilled. He did not wish to make an enquiry about his family, or otherwise he might attract questioning by some Party official about himself; who he really was and what exactly he had been doing during the long period of the wars.

As it was, once he had joined the Party – as all who sought employment now must do – surprisingly few questions were asked of him, and those that were he was able to answer with an imaginative mixture of fact and half-truths that he hoped disguised the reality behind them.

He used his real name of Detrichen. It was a common enough surname, in any event: there were probably hundreds of other Detrichens in the City. Workers were usually only known by their surnames in the Party, unless you rose to a much more senior rank, so his distinctive forename of Albanus was not in question. He had merely put a capital K before Detrichen on the forms he had had to fill in. If anyone asked, he was Kurt, again a very common name. But few ever did.

He waited anxiously for a further more rigorous examination, but it never came. The amnesty had been coupled with a general policy of reconciliation, which, given the brutality of the Party rule to date, was also surprising. But what the Party required now amongst their resettled peoples – or so Albanus reasoned – was education, in particular literacy and numeracy skills, an average competence in these at the least, to be ascertained by a quick testing.

He had passed his short, written exam easily, and the result was good enough to gain him his job as a Party clerk. Of course, he could probably have got a simple labouring job rather more easily, and with even less questioning, but such jobs were much less well-paid and often highly dangerous, and came without any accommodation other than a bunk space in a hostel. So, despite his initial repulsion at the idea of working for his former enemy, this was the course he had decided upon, now that he was finished with fighting.

His past – he was never asked to provide details of the soldiering he had done, although he admitted to having fought at the beginning of the war, as all young men had been conscripted to do – seemed to have been written off under the amnesty, to be tolerated as of little relevance now, providing he never offended again. If he did, then a distant labour camp hidden away in the frozen regions of the northern mountains, would likely be where he would see out the remainder of his days. It was said that those sent there had a life expectancy of only a year.

Albanus wished most fervently to live. He had seen enough of death. He wanted to enjoy life again, although, as he soon found out, there was little of that on offer in the City now. Did he regret coming to the City then? He didn't think so. It had been a question of finding a life of any sort, instead of a certain death. He knew that as a militia soldier he could not have survived longer than another few months or so. There are only so many chances a soldier is given, and he had used up his luck a long time ago.

When the hooter sounded for the end of the working day – hooters wailed out often in the City, different calls for different purposes, so the air was usually filled with some long, howling tone or other – Albanus would join the queues at the doors that led out into the streets, punching out the time on one of the old-fashioned clocking machines that were still in use. Then he would join the long, drab boiler-suited streams heading towards the centre of the City, where a few trams ran or ancient buses with exhausts emitting clouds of black gases.

'Anything yer got on tonight, sir?' one of his juniors might ask, attempting a friendship perhaps that might provide a greater security for himself. A clerk's superior acted like a king in his own small domain, but that system in turn extended upwards, so no one was ever secure from sudden dismissal, with little reason given, and that unchallengeable.

'Nothing much' was his invariable answer. He preferred to be by himself. Very occasionally he would join a group of senior clerks going to one of the drink halls, where they would get through most of their weekly pay drinking the *ghraushitz'* – the 'rough shit' that was otherwise labelled as vodka. It was made, they said, from potato peelings laced with the industrial alcohol used in the revolving turrets of tanks: it peeled the skin from the roof of the mouth. What it did to your internal organs, he could only guess at. He had seen a dead man being carried out of drinking den one evening. He had only tasted *ghraushitz* once, and that was enough: he usually stuck to the weak beer, or watered down wine, that were otherwise on offer – the latter said to be flavoured with the piss of the country girls who trampled the grapes.

Most evenings he would go to one of the Party canteens that lined the bottom end of the 'Road of Victory'. This ran from the old cathedral – now used as a temporary Party headquarters, and soon to be demolished, its many spires had already been taken down, some said by artillery practice – and up a long, gently-sloping hill to where the white stone facade of the new Presidential Palace glittered in the sunlight, surrounded by its many marbled pools and jetting fountains.

In the Party canteen – Albanus was seated at a table there now – subsidised for Party workers only, he could get a reasonable meal, often with meat, for a price he could afford, if he only eat properly once a day. And here as well, he could hope to meet with women fellow workers – clerks, machinists, brick-layers, nurses, tram-drivers, they all used this canteen, often as lonely as he and desperately seeking a man's company, although they usually came with entanglements of the type he did not want. Or available also might be a number of those powdered and scented girls whose approaches to the men were much more professional, a practice to which the Party seemed to turn a blind eye. This latter category, he preferred, although it would mean a small extra cost he could ill afford.

His favourite girl, whom he hoped would be present this evening, was Icheka. He had known her for some months and had given her his real forename, Albanus. He thought there was little risk in doing this, and he didn't like the moans of 'Oh, Kurt' while in the throws of passion.

Icheka worked at the hospital and was training to be a nurse. She came from a small village in the mountains: her father had been a shepherd there until one day he and much of his flock had been machine-gunned from the air by a helicopter gun crew just out 'enjoying themselves.' Her mother had died of a heart attack from the shock. Now Icheka supplemented her very small income with an occasional evening of prostitution, or on rare occasions – if the money was very good – a full night.

And so Albanus sat lingering over his greasy plate of food, nursing the gravelly beer in his plastic mug – gravelly because it still contained floating fragments of the black-husked grain from which it had been brewed. I'd have to drink a gallon at least to get even remotely pissed, he thought, and by then my insides would probably be destroyed, anyway.

Someone he knew on another table flung across to him a copy of the 'Party News'. It was a broad-leafed newspaper of only a few sheets. On the front page beneath a flaring headline that stated 'Final Victory is Ours' (how many times had Albanus seen that over the years, but it did seem this time it might be coming true), there was a small item lower down that caught his eye: it was headed 'Christian Poison'.

He read: 'The Party has tolerated the poison of Christianity for far too long. It spreads mischief and falsehood wherever it goes. The State President, in an informal speech at his summer home to veteran Party members, stated: 'For years we have been as tolerant as possible of this superstition, as we know it sustained many of our people in their struggles for liberation in former times; so we have been magnanimous in allowing private ceremonies to be carried out, although any form of public worship or propaganda has for some time been strictly forbidden. We are minded now, however, to ban Christianity entirely. Our decrees on this matter, and the severe penalties for any found in breach of them, will shortly be announced".

Albanus looked at the date of the newspaper: it was some three months old. So, he thought, are those decrees now in force? Is Christianity banned everywhere, in or out of one's home? And he found himself thinking again of the priest Amphibalus in his black cassock and his hooded, leather cape. The priest had been so confident of the rightness of his journeying with him, indeed a certitude of it, that Albanus had felt sure he would see him again as he continued his journey from Janita and that stricken farm towards the City, sleeping out each night in the fields and cadging food from farms – but the priest had never appeared.

Perhaps that great lout at the farm had died, and the priest no longer sought the company of his murderer – but he didn't really think that was the case. Had not he seen the fallen man coming round? Anyhow, he had acted purely in self-defence. It would have been he who was killed, if his reaction had been a fraction of a second slower.

Strange as it might seem, Albanus had to confess to a slight disappointment about the priest's non-appearance, for he had gained a respect for him, having seen at first hand the comfort he brought to the suffering people. Now it was too late. He had joined his former enemy – the Party. He was sure the priest would never come to him again.

But to interrupt his thoughts most delightfully, here was Icheka now, weaving her small body between the rows of tables, watched by the fascinated eyes of many boiler-suited workers, women as well as men, the looks of the women more of envy than desire. Same sex relationships were little tolerated by the Party.

Icheka was wearing a boiler suit that she herself had re-tailored to make it much more figure hugging than the official version, which usually had a sack-like appearance at the very best. Female nurses were forbidden to wear their own attractive uniforms beyond the hospital gates, and any caught doing so, in particular for an 'unsavoury purpose', would undoubtedly have got them instantly sacked, and likely sent to a labour camp.

Albanus did not really care what Icheka was wearing. He was just happy to see her. She slid onto the seat beside him at the table, and he caught a whiff of her perfume, which must have come from some expensive source – possibly a satisfied senior Party official, he thought.

'Have you eaten? Can I get you anything?' he asked, knowing his ration was almost spent.

She shook her head. Her short blonde hair bounced enticingly, catching the light from the bare electric bulb immediately overhead. Growing long hair was frowned upon for most women after the first cutting was made of a young girl. All hair cuttings either went to the munitions factories to bind the shell cases, or the more attractive lengths to the wig makers for the ladies of the higher officials.

'I ate at the hospital,' Icheka said. 'I'll have a cup of tea, though.'

He fetched her that in a stained plastic beaker, all he could find. Tea at least was off-ration and free in this canteen.

They did not stay long. Icheka told him she wanted him to meet some friends of hers. He wondered who they were. Not members of some sordid sex group, he hoped. He had heard about such goings on, despite the Party's 'purity laws'.

They came out of the canteen's front door into the street. This was not an evening he would have to pay her for, she told him, taking his hand, and pulling him between the clanking trams onto the opposite pavement. She would say no more and Albanus was content to go along with her.

Then suddenly, as they turned into the Road of Victory, she stopped, pressing close to him. 'I'm ashamed of what I've done – being a tart, I mean. I swear, I'll do no more of it!' Her eyes were filled with tears.

He was disbelieving of her. She had spoken like this several times before, but always she had returned to her evening trade. She had needed the money, she had told him. The price of everything was rising steeply. Yet now she did sound much more certain. Albanus's first reaction was one of annoyance, selfish as he knew that to be. She had been a good friend, as well as satisfying his physical needs. He did not want to lose her.

They crossed the river that flowed through the City, then turned in and out of several side streets, all fronted by high, concrete apartment blocks, similar to Albanus's own, but perhaps even more mean-looking, with laundry draped out of windows and with many white and grey satellite dishes stuck on their facades like a spreading fungus. At last, Icheka stopped at an entrance door of frosted glass that was cracked and bedaubed with graffiti. She pushed it open. Albanus found he was in a small, dirty hallway which smelt of urine.

'We won't use the lift,' she hissed at Albanus. 'It's unsafe, and people have been stuck for days. I was told the other day of a man found dead in a broken-down lift.'

Hell, thought Albanus. Why is she bringing me to a rundown place like this? Is it safe? I should get out of here. Albanus's hard-earned survival instincts as a soldier were re-emerging.

He called out his concern to her, but she was ahead of him now on the stairs, and it seemed impossible for him just to let her go and not to follow. Likely, he would never see her again. Where on earth was she taking him? He should pull away now. It had to be something more than simple lust for her, or even just plain friendship, that made him keep going. There was something about the conviction of what she had just told him and her clear determination now that caused him to abandon his usual caution. And so he continued up the stairs behind her.

They mounted flight after flight, never passing anyone, seeing long corridors stretching away on each floor, with much litter scattered about – old bikes, old prams, plastic bags of rubbish, discarded bottles and cans. He thought his own apartment block was poor, but it was like a sweet dream compared with this nightmare of a place. He asked her again where they were going, but she did not answer, just hurried on.

They came to yet another landing, and this time Icheka stopped and checked a board screwed crookedly to the wall, which showed the flat numbers of the floor.

'Nearly there,' she said, looking back at him as he mounted the final stair, considerably out of breath. Other than for a flush of her cheeks, she seemed untroubled by the long climb. She is fitter than me, he thought wonderingly. And once I was fitter than the sleek rats I shared the trenches with.

They set off down a corridor. 'I recognise it now,' Icheka said. 'I've only been here once before, you see.'

'Who are we meeting with?'

'You'll soon find out.' That was not the answer he wanted. He was growing cross with her now. He either turned straightaway and left, or he accepted the situation. He continued following her. His skin began to prickle, though, as his senses were freshly alerted. Trust no one – trust nothing at all – had been his motto.

At last Icheka halted at a door. It was painted blue, but the paint had bubbled up and was peeling off. There was a rusty letter box at its centre (he doubted if any letter carrier actually ever came here), and the number in black plastic figures – 2337. One of the 3s was tilted sideways. A buzzer was set in the wall at one side. When Icheka pressed it, no sound could be heard. She pressed it again. Eventually, Albanus heard the patter of feet approaching? He tensed. He carried no weapon. Only the army and the police were allowed weapons. A citizen could be prosecuted for carrying even a cosh. How reckless he had been in following Icheka here so blindly, not knowing what was to come.

He heard a bolt being drawn back, and the door swung open. A woman of middle years stood there. She had black hair, cut in a pudding basin style, and large black eyes.

'Icheka! You said you'd come. And this is...?'

'The friend I told you of.'

'Oh yes. Do come in.' She smiled a welcome at Albanus. 'My name is Nanta. I am so pleased to meet you. We are all gathered in the back room. The priest is with us, Icheka!'

Albanus saw Icheka's hand fly to her mouth. She exclaimed: 'So he *has* come, as you said he would. How wonderful!'

'Yes, the rumours turned out true. We have our priest at last! He has long been travelling to us. He arrived just a week ago. And he is to stay here for the present.' She laughed. 'It is lucky I keep a spare room'

Coming out of an inner door towards them, Albanus saw through his bewilderment the well-remembered black cassock and leather cape, the arms opened wide, the dark, bearded face, and he heard again the booming voice:

'So Albanus, once more we meet – dear Albanus whom I had thought was lost, God has allowed me to find my lost sheep. And the good woman who has brought him to me – Icheka, as I understand. You are both most welcome to join us. We shall worship the Christ and give praise to him, for it is he who has watched over us and brought us together once more in this house.'

7

Albanus was astonished. As he recovered from the shock of seeing the priest again – dangerous to him very possibly, as the priest knew of his past and of the many killings he had made of that enemy he now sought to be at peace with – anger began to fill him. Why was this man, with his fanciful talk of eternal life, always at his heels? And how on earth had he found him in the City, which must surely be the place of greatest danger for a priest – one too who apparently went about undisguised – given the new decrees against any teaching of his God, or Christ, or whatever other name might be used for his deity now?

After a grunt of a greeting to the priest, who must surely have realised his displeasure, Albanus was tempted to leave straightaway, and leave Icheka too, whom he had so foolishly allowed to bring him here. What was her purpose, she a friend but a prostitute too?

Or – he had the sudden crazed thought – was that, in fact, exactly what this was all about, as he had suspected earlier, some sort of communal activity that involved sex? Was this, oh so pure and sinless Christianity, in fact a religion in which its adherents worked themselves up into sexual frenzy? He seemed to remember hearing stories like that about godly hypocrites when he was a soldier, but had discounted them as merely malicious tales, put out by the unholy when confronted by the smugness of the righteous.

As quickly as this thought came to him, he realised how ridiculous it was – foolish and insulting too. He remembered the priest at the farm where they had stayed, and the happiness of the people who had come over the fields to be blessed by him, and he felt immediately ashamed of himself. And he thought again of Janita, whom he had long dismissed from his mind, and realised how sincere she had been in her faith. She was incapable of anything evil or morally repugnant: his earlier brief suspicion that she had aided her brother in his attack on him he had long since dismissed, feeling sick with himself for even having thought it.

Janita's desire to follow him to the City had been cruelly overturned. She would not be able to seek him out now, even if she were still minded to do so: the address he had scrawled for her so hastily and hopefully that terrible evening was now to a building site.

Instead of leaving this gathering, however, as his reason told him to do, he found himself following the others into a large room, where a dining table had been pushed back against one of the walls to make an open space. Here a number of people, perhaps ten men and women, young and elderly, were seated on chairs arranged in a rough half circle. Two more men stood against a wide window that looked out at the concrete corner of the apartment block opposite, under a sky that was already darkening into night. Nanta was even now pulling the curtains across.

As there were no more chairs, Icheka squatted down amongst cushions on the floor, while Albanus, wishing to remain on his feet, shuffled discontentedly to a place next to one of the men by the window.

The priest, who had now removed his cape so that the wooden cross with its white, hanging figure of the crucified god could be seen against his black cassock, stood before the group, with the door behind him and a small table in front. On the table was placed his silver chalice and a white china plate upon which was a round loaf of bread. There's no escape for me now then, Albanus thought, with a shiver of alarm; the only way out of here would have to be through the priest's own body.

The priest begun by asking those present to introduce themselves. Nanta, whose flat this was, gave them greeting, stating, 'I am baptised in Christ'. Others then spoke similarly, giving their names – Johan, Bessita, Khyren, Pietrus, Sjamden...... and others too – all stating they were 'servants of Christ'. Pietunia next declared herself a 'follower of Christ', as did several others, including, to Albanus's surprise, Icheka.

How long has she been such? he wondered, cynically. Does she not find that following this Christ gets in the way of her usual evening activity? She has let me down badly by bringing me here. She and I are finished, he determined. But immediately he felt such a flood of sadness at the thought that he knew he would be unable to carry out this resolution.

When the priest looked at Albanus to give his name, he shook his head. If he gives it for me – or Icheka does for that matter – then I *will* leave straightaway, even if I have to shoulder my way out. Just being here could get me arrested, and then the Party might investigate me somewhat more thoroughly than they did before, and the new life I have sought will be over – perhaps literally.

The priest, however, simply passed on. When the naming was complete, he said 'For you who do not know me already, I am Amphibalus, a priest of Christ. I will give you news of our master, Jesus Christ, of how we can worship him in this our congregation, and of how we may bring others to our faith, despite the dangers that are now placed before us. But for the present I wish you all to give thanks to God for the blessings he has brought to us, so we are able to give praise to him here in the house of Nanta. Let us pray.'

All who were seated rose to their feet, their arms outstretched before them. To his complete surprise, Albanus found himself doing the same, almost as if his body was compelling him into actions that his mind otherwise refused to accept. What I do here now means nothing, he assured himself, but either I leave this place entirely or I must conform to some degree, otherwise I will stand out like a sore thumb. And that will only make things worse for me and very likely upset the others here too, to whom I wish no harm at all.

He was still angry, though, that he had been put into this position. At the farm those months back he had been but an observer: he had felt no desire then to take part in the priest's rituals, nor had anyone compelled him to do so. But, very strangely, he felt his attitude changing now, if only by a degree or so. Part of him still didn't wish to be here at all, yet another part, possibly the greater part, was curious enough not simply to dismiss outright what he saw and heard taking place. It was a realisation of some surprise to him, having been so hostile only minutes earlier. There had been, a tussle, he tried to reason, between his conscious and unconscious minds.

After the prayers had been said, and the responses made, during which Albanus had remained silent – he did not know the words to use, in any event – all those with chairs re-seated themselves. Albanus saw Icheka settling herself amongst her cushions, then turn her head to find him standing by the window, giving him a smile. He acknowledged her by a raising of his hand, but his face remained bleak. Whatever changes might be going on inside him, he was not going to show even a hint of them outwardly.

The priest addressed them. He told them of the new dangers they faced as Christians under the further restrictions of the Party's rule.

'Some of us will be persecuted,' he said, 'some will suffer for our faith, but you are all part of God's kingdom now, and he will be by your side. Keep that before you should the hour of trial be visited upon you. God is with you *always*. You have but to call upon him and your pain will be eased. He offers us eternal life, and it will be glorious when we are called to him to pass into the heaven he holds open for us.'

'Yet, for the present time, you should not be foolish in the way you spread his holy word. Be careful of speaking of Christ to those whom you do not at first recognise, those who ask for information about you – of who you are, and how and where you worship, and of the others who worship with you. Invite only those you judge to be genuine enquirers after the truth – those to whom you would wish to spread the good news of our father – to come to some private, trusted place, as we are here today. And remember that I will be moving often amongst you all to give you God's blessing, and to make witness with you of Christ's own sacrifice for us, by his own blood and flesh now risen in glory, which we celebrate by the taking of bread and wine, as he showed us before his own great suffering. And so we do this now.'

One after another, many of the congregation – but not Icheka, Albanus noted – came up to the table and sipped from the chalice into which the priest had poured wine from the jug, and took into their mouths a piece of the bread he held out to them, while he gave them God's blessing. Then silently the room emptied, by groups of two at irregular intervals, Nanta undertaking the direction of this, with the opening and closing of the outer door to the flat.

Albanus assumed this procedure was so as not to arouse any undue suspicion from neighbours who might be watching; some hope that, he thought wryly, his anxieties as to his own safety sharply renewed. Eventually he was left alone with the priest. Icheka had disappeared with Nanta into another room. He had the strong feeling that this had been pre-arranged. Yet, why exactly?

Despite his earlier spark of interest, his unease at this situation was growing again. Why couldn't he be left alone to find his own way to their god, if that indeed was ever something he would wish? He rounded on the priest now, confronting him in a corner of the room, and speaking to him in a low, angry voice.

'How did you find me, sir priest? How dare you do so and have me brought here, when you must realise any connection of mine with you now might bring me into danger.'

'I did not seek you out,' he answered steadily. 'I have done nothing myself to have you brought to me. Yet, it has happened, as I always knew it would. God's purpose with you was clear to me from the time I first met you. I know you will not believe me, Albanus – not yet, anyhow – and you will think me just an interfering priest who peddles nonsense for his own gratification – but you will come to understand that you have been chosen by God for a purpose – and so it will happen. Even if I wished differently, there is nothing I can do about it. The others who were here are true followers of the faith: they believe in God and trust him. You have yet to believe as they do, but your faith will come, it will come.....'

'You have talked to me in such riddles before, sir priest. It is nonsense. Now I am one of the chosen ones, indeed! What rubbish you speak! I do not believe in your god and never will. You must find other things – other people – to concern yourself with, not me. What is so special about me, anyhow?

All I seek now are some years of peace that I can enjoy. I have had enough of serving other people's causes to my own great loss. Are these small hopes of mine then but the sins of which you Christians speak? Your inventions about me must be for your own reasons. I cannot imagine why. Please find someone else to play your games with. They are crazed. Perhaps it is you who are crazed, sir priest. I wish nothing more to do with you. Do I make that clear?'

'And yet I saw how you prayed with the others just now.' The priest raised his hands and laid them on Albanus's shoulders, who did not pull away. 'You are steadfast and brave. We Christians need men like you amongst us.'

'I stood with the others and made a pretence of joining in as I had no seat and there was nothing else I could do, unless I walked out – and that might have been dangerous, not only for me personally but for all of you here. I imagine the outer door was locked. Breaking it down might have created some attention, don't you think? You see, I don't wish any of you harm. I only work for the Party in order to live. I hate them as much as I ever did when I was fighting them.'

'It is love you need, Albanus. Your need for hate, which kept you alive during the war, has passed.' The priest chuckled, much to Albanus's surprise. 'I don't mean the love of a woman, either, although in that you are probably successful.'

'No', he added quickly, seeing the displeasure on Albanus's face, 'I mean that in the conquest of evil, love is essential.'

Against his instincts to end the conversation there and then and escape from here as soon as possible, Albanus felt compelled to question the priest's last statement.

'What do you mean, priest? How can you hope to be rid of a vicious enemy by loving him? That has to be the maddest fairytale of all. He laughed sardonically. 'You keep telling me them, don't you? Is your Christianity made up of fantasies like that? If so, you must live in a dream world rather than a real one.'

'Albanus...' The priest's hands were still on his shoulders and surprisingly he felt no desire to shake them off; rather, he found them fatherly, even consoling. How was that? This man must be working a magic over him in the same way that he clearly bewitched others.

'Albanus,' the priest spoke his name again. 'Our Lord, Jesus Christ, the Son of God, told us, we should love our enemy. Christians have tried to follow this commandment ever since. In ancient Rome – a civilisation of which your father taught, as you have told me – many thousands, tens of thousands, died doing just that in the persecutions the Roman authorities brought down on them, yet in time their faith, their strength, grew to be that of Rome herself: the cross of Christ was placed upon the banners of all her armies. Such a transformation can only be achieved through the greatest power of all – that of love – so those who hate us now can be brought in time through God's love to Christ himself.'

'Again you talk in riddles, priest.'

But he felt less sure now. He remembered his father telling him of the rule of the ancient Romans. The god of the Christians – the one they called the son of man – had been born at a time and a place ruled by Rome's cruel authority, surely similar to that which prevails in this State today. But Christianity had come to rule Rome, as the priest had told. How had that been possible?

The priest said, lowering his voice and speaking directly into Albanus's ear, his bearded face brushing his, 'Christ was seized by his enemies, condemned and crucified. He died on the cross, but rose from the dead and ascended into heaven. He gives strength to all who believe in him. All things become possible if you only have faith and call upon Christ to help you. All kingdoms, fortifications, and armies, those powers built by the flesh and bone that is man, will crumble away before his supreme power of love. Rather, Albanus, think of love – that love which is the spirit of life – and not so much of hate, which only brings yet more hatred and pain and misery.'

'You have seen me kill, priest. How can I then think of love? Does your god of love have a purpose and a place for killers?'

'He has a place and a purpose for everyone, Albanus, if you do truly repent and turn to him.'

'I cannot repent of the killing I have done. It was necessary at the time, and those I killed would have killed me if they had been able to do so first. Yet, I do wish, above all, that I had not had to do those things. What then would be my place with your god?

'I cannot answer for sure. Yet I know that if you truly love God, then all will become clear to you.'

Albanus laughed, a horrible grating sound in which he scarce recognised himself. 'You are all words, priest. You muddle my brain with them. For the present I want no more.'

'But you will return?' The priest's voice held hope.

'How could I, even if I wished that? It is dangerous here. We are all likely to be caught by the Party's security police, you in particular. It appears you walk about openly as a priest. How long do you think it will last before you are arrested?"

'I stay here for now. When the time comes to leave I shall do so in darkness.'

'But you could easily be recognised by your dress, however dark the night may be, and by your beard too. Not many Party members wear beards.'

'I walk with the Lord.'

Albanus was growing annoyed again now. 'Yes, that is all very well, but you will endanger those about you too.'

'The Lord will show the way.'

The priest locked his gaze on Albanus, eye to eye, and he realised his complete sincerity. He believed absolutely in what he said – yet surely he was foolhardy and selfish in doing so – selfish inasmuch as he would allow others to be caught and punished by the Party, even if he did not care what happened to himself.

But now the priest was smiling at him. 'You are perplexed, Albanus. I see that. If you would only come to our faith and bind its strength about you, then you would think differently. I shall be as careful as I can, I assure you. Though, perhaps you are right. I should cut off my beard.' He gave a deep grunt of laughter, stroking his chin. 'I will not feel the same without it.'

'It may not be enough,' Albanus said testily.

Surely, he thought, you can be strong in your beliefs, yet be sensible for your safety at the same time. It did not seem an impossible concession to make. It surely did not undermine your faith. What was the point of suffering at the hands of those who hated you unless that really was the only way, there being no other? To do so was simply stupidity.

While he was thinking these things, Icheka appeared suddenly from an inner room, looking up anxiously into his face. She must be aware of his arguing with the priest.

'Is all well?' she asked, smiling uncertainly.

'Yes,' Albanus replied decisively. 'Come we must leave now, or I must go by myself, should you wish to stay.'

'I am ready to come with you,' she said at once.

'I will think on what you have told me', Albanus said, turning back to the priest, who bowed his head in acknowledgement.

'I know you will, my son. I will pray that I see you again soon.'

Albanus felt Icheka's eyes on him, dark pools of light, hopeful, appealing.

'Right, I *will* come again,' he heard himself say, but he did not really believe it.

He did not want to lose Icheka,. Not now, most certainly, although earlier he had thought she had deceived him. Would this new Christian Icheka be someone quite different? He wanted the old Icheka to stay, the one who made him laugh and gave him companionship, and satisfied his body.

Did Christianity allow such feelings, or were they too much of the flesh and not the spirit? Not all Christians were saints. Some surely were simply human beings, seeking hope in a most troubled world. He recognised he was one such. Whether he shared their religion, or not, these Christians, he had to admit, were at least interesting people. They have a passion for humanity, and a respect for the individual, far removed from the conformity the Party would stamp upon all of us. Perhaps then....but he did not wish to think any further along those lines for the moment.

He and Icheka made their farewells to the priest, and to Nanta who had come to the door to see them off. It was now dark outside. Only the occasional dim lamp shone on the long landings and the stairway. They picked their way carefully down the stairs. To Albanus's relief they passed no one and reached the street outside, where the earlier heavy traffic flow had largely ceased. Only the occasional lorry or car passed them in yellow pools of light.

Coming to the river bridge, he led Icheka down a flight of steps to a concrete platform that connected two of the bridge piles. There was just enough of a glow from the street lamps above for them to see. He had been here with her before when she had been practising her trade, but now he did not know how willing she would be. Yet, she abandoned herself to him with a passion she had scarcely shown before when money had been involved. They clung together for some time, smelling the rotting odour of the river sliding beneath them into the blackness.

'You will see me again?' he asked.

'Of course.' He could see her smile in the dark by the gleam of her teeth and her shining eyes.

'Then call for me in a week, as you have done tonight.'

'Where will we go? I would like...'

'I know,' he said, kissing her lips, then placing his finger upon them. 'I will return to the priest, as I told him.'

'You believe then?'

'I am curious.'

'It is enough, perhaps.'

She took his finger into her mouth and bit at it, which roused him to take her once more. The moon had risen and was high in the sky when he got back to his flat. He lay for a while sleepless, wondering what was happening to him – this former soldier for whom simple survival had once been everything.

8

In fact, it was to be more than three months before Albanus saw Icheka again, a period of winter frosts and snows, which made it hard to get about in the City. Quite out of the blue, four days after his reacquaintance with the priest at Nanta's flat, he was informed by his immediate Party supervisor that he was to be promoted. This was not to be within his present department, however, but at another entirely – the Department of Procurement – where his principal work would be concerned with food requisition and supply. It would mean a move to a newly built Party office at the outer edge of the most northerly suburb of the City. With the promotion came better accommodation too – a small, box-like house, not far from his new office, on an estate built recently and close to open countryside. He was expected to move there and take up his new role within a few short weeks.

In all the upheaval this involved for him, including a week at a Party training college where he slept in a dormitory with other Party workers recently promoted, he put to the back of his mind all thoughts about Icheka, the priest, and everything else he had seen and felt that last time he had been with them. With his training over and his move to his new house completed, it was only now that, with a guilty start, he thought of Icheka sitting in the canteen where they used to meet waiting for him each evening, and then walking away, perhaps full of sadness, when he did not show up as he had told her he would.

Perhaps, though, he pondered, she has met someone else by now and gone back to her old ways. He hoped very much that was not true, but he continued to be so caught up in his new job that he had no time to feel too much sorrow or concern on the matter. It was all a great shame, because she had been so lovely that last evening with the priest, and afterwards, and so excited about her new beliefs which she had wanted him to share.

And, despite his earlier outward scorn and anger, he knew that, deep within him, what he had witnessed then, and been told by the priest, had made an impression – if he was truthful, in fact, rather more than an impression. For a moment indeed, something had begun to grow within him. He had felt it, he knew – however unlikely that had seemed at the time, and certainly did now. He knew he had wanted to learn more, and that his hostility at first had been but a reaction to defend himself, more out of fear than anything else – a fear that he would lose his job as a result, or worse. Now, with his promotion and his move, what he had learnt that evening was largely forgotten, as if it had never happened – yet not quite.

His new responsibilities brought him a fresh determination to succeed in his work, although he still hated the Party, and, in truth, disliked himself for being so weak as to fall in with it for his own advantage. Would it not have been more honourable to accept the battlefield death that would certainly have come to him, however futile that might have been?

Yet, he had made his decision, and this new work for the Party he must do to his fullest ability. He consoled himself that at least the job was one that would help the people, and not make their lives more miserable or bring them into danger. He soon had his team organised. He had his own office with his name on the door: it had a large picture window looking out over fields and woods, now shining white under the thick snows that had fallen.

His house had not taken long to organise. He had so few possessions it required only one Party-paid taxi trip on icy roads to move them there from his former flat. He was entitled to a supply of Party-issued furniture, and a small-screen television providing access to the two Party-controlled channels, all of which arrived one day when he was at the office and were left dumped outside on the small, frozen front lawn. He was able to arrange everything to his satisfaction the next day, and to set up the television so that it worked, in which he was aided by his neighbour from the house next door – a female titan of considerable girth whose hair was bound up into pigtails: he felt quite unable to repay her in the manner she hinted at. After that, he had few dealings with her and only saw her at a distance, when she would usually turn her back on him. He was glad. Away from the office, he wanted to keep very much to himself.

However, being now more senior in the Party, he was aware that he should become involved with at least one or two of its social activities that were advertised on the circulars coming regularly to him. If he did not, he knew he would stand out as a loner, or even a misfit, and that would not be good for him. Lack of Party sociability, at the very least might prevent further promotion; at the worst, it might mean questions being asked about him. He certainly did not want that.

When the snows had melted and the days were warmer, with the first signs of spring beginning to appear, he decided to join a Party shooting club. He soon realised this was a mistake. Many of the members had served in the State army, and he soon became involved in convoluted fabrications about himself and what he had been doing during the war. As his skill with the weapons, single shot and automatic, being fired on the club's ranges was so obvious, he was questioned further by a jocular, hard-drinking bunch in the club bar afterwards, and was glad to get away with his various stories not penetrated too seriously. He did not return.

Instead he joined a more ordinary social group at the Party's principal leisure club in the centre of the City. Here, he was troubled by no more than a passing question about his work or his vacation plans – a lodge on the great Inner Lake was recommended to him. He eat at the club occasionally and was friendly with a few he met – table tennis was a game he learnt – but otherwise kept much to himself. Often he would go to the club's cinema, where he watched censored feature films imported from overseas, or slept through locally-produced documentaries about bee-keeping, personal fitness, car maintenance, cookery, and the history of the Party's rise to power.

It was after viewing such a film one evening, when coming from the darkened auditorium into the brightly-lit lounge outside, that he saw Icheka. She was seated at a low table with a Party official in full uniform beside her. His uniform was of a blue cloth decorated with much gold braid and medal ribbons, set off by a huge round, peaked cap. Even as a shocked Albanus hurriedly bent his body away, hoping not to be seen, the official removed the cap, revealing a balding scalp of straggling grey hair. When at the outer door of the room, Albanus looked back, it was to see Icheka staring at him, as if transfixed, while the official, apparently unaware of her fixation elsewhere, continued his talk with her. She had seen and recognised him, for certain.

Desperate to speak to her, but not here in front of this Party officer, he sat down at an empty table by the door, so her back was now to him, and kept a watch on them. Eventually, they rose and left together, she intent on her companion. She did not even glance around to see if Albanus was still there. He felt a great pang of disappointment. He waited on, however, hoping against hope that she would return – and, after a time, just as he was about to give up his waiting, to his very great pleasure, she did.

With a bright smile, Icheka slid onto the chair beside him. She was wearing a long dress of a shiny green material, patterned with white flowers. A golden pendant hung at the creamy white of her throat. He saw her nails were painted a bright red, matching her lipstick. Her blonde hair, longer now, had been carefully styled, piled up fashionably and falling down at the sides in ringlets.

This was a new Icheka. To have been allowed such decoration of her person, she must have been favoured in some way by the Party. She could not have achieved such an expensive appearance on her nurse's pay. So had she returned to her former trade, he wondered, but at a superior level – a mistress perhaps to some senior Party official? What of her Christianity then? Had that been just a short-lived wonder for her, a brief experiment, which she had abandoned as soon as a better prospect had come along?

He kept his voice level and non-committal: 'What work are you doing now?' he asked. 'Are you still at the hospital?'

'Yes', she answered, rather to his surprise. She had no look of guilt or embarrassment about her. 'But I've been recruited by the Party's Exterior Relations Department to work for them as well. It's only part time, as and when I'm needed. But the extra pay is very good. I also get a clothes allowance. You see, I accompany foreign visitors about, make them feel at home, explain the way things work here, that sort of thing. And *nothing more.*'

She added the last with emphasis, seeing Albanus's look. It was said in such a frank, guileless way that he immediately believed her and felt sorry for his earlier suspicions. A wave of relief flooded through him.

'The man you saw me with', she went on – more sure of herself now she had passed over the hurdle of his scrutiny: yet, he thought with some concern, perhaps she tells me more than she should – 'he is from a Calpuchasian legation that is visiting at present. I have spent the afternoon showing him some of the City and its new buildings – the museum and the art gallery, he found very interesting. He is to be driven next to meet the State President at a banquet at the Presidential Palace tonight. But I've finished my role with him for now.'

Albanus knew something of Calpuchasia. It lay to the east of their own territory and had long supplied arms and other support to the Party. Despite his new palace in the City, the State President normally met visitors at his mountain retreat, where these days he spent much of his time. It was the first Albanus had heard of his presence in the City again, despite the innumerable Party messages and other communiqués that passed over his desk. Security, of course, needed to be very tight. So he felt a pang of concern for Icheka for so casually breaking it. Who else might be listening to them? He glanced around. There was no one close enough to have done so.

Keeping his voice as low as he could, as it would certainly not be good to be overheard on this matter, and he was far from certain there were not hidden cameras or listening devices here in the walls or ceiling, he asked: 'Have you seen the priest recently?'

'Yes', she answered, surprising him. He had thought that with the excitement of her new job – and indeed with the extra security vetting it must have demanded – her Christian inclinations might have evaporated as quickly as they had appeared.

'I saw him and the others two nights ago. He was asking about you.'

'Where is he now?'

'At the same place – Nanta's flat – where you saw him with me.'

'Is it not dangerous for you to go there? Even more so, given your new role with the Party.'

She stuck her chin out obstinately. 'Yes, but it is worth it. I do what our Lord instructs me in prayer. I am very careful.'

'You will need to be. And the priest, how is he?'

'He keeps very well. He never wavers. He is our strength and our hope.'

'Does he leave the flat?'

'I think so. He comes and goes at night, I believe'.

'If they catch him, they will likely kill him. So you see the danger you put yourself in.'

'He has shaved off his beard.'

Oh, so he has done that, Albanus thought. Perhaps he will now leave off that cape of his too and wear other clothes.

'As for my own safety,' Icheka added, 'I trust in God.'

'That may not be enough,' Albanus said. 'Please be very careful and look after yourself.'

She looked him in the eyes, resolute, defiant. 'Will you come to see the priest again? Or are you too scared?'

He did not rise to the bait. 'If I don't come, it is not because I fear,' he said slowly. 'It is because I do not believe. Yet', he added, 'there is a power about that man – that is for sure – and a wonder too, that tells me I do not wish never to see him again. Indeed, if I'm honest, despite my uncertainty at what he preaches, he *pulls* at me, like a scrap of iron is drawn to a magnet, in a way I do not understand.'

'So, you will come with me again?'

'Yes, Icheka, I will.'

He did not quite believe his own words, but they were said now. After all, he *had* made that promise to the priest those long weeks ago. Yet, was he more intent on being with her again than with the priest? He didn't know. It was a combination of several things, he thought, that made the risk worthwhile.

'It'll be at Nanta's flat.'

'It's dangerous going there,' he said. 'I suppose it's the only possible place. In three days time, I shall be free in the evening.'

He had already told her how he too had come up in the Party and had his own small house now at the edge of the City. 'Where shall we meet up beforehand?' he asked.

'How about here at the club? I can contact Nanta and make the arrangements. She will be so happy I've found you again.'

'That's fine. What time? Shall we say around seven? The walk is only a mile or so.'

And so it was agreed.

9

Albanus's sympathies with these Christians, whom fate had placed him amongst, grew quickly, but what first began to ease his stubbornness about their beliefs is harder to identify. Perhaps it was the sight of others of the congregation, in the small compass of Nanta's room standing with arms outstretched, a few on their knees, all so utterly believing, intent on their prayer, that eased him into his own conversion. They spoke the sacred words in unison with the priest, while Albanus, at the back of the room, stood alone in the coldness of his spirit, separate from them by his inability to join in. He visited Nanta's flat to join the priest in worship several times during the next weeks, and gradually this coldness changed to greater warmth, and then into a much fuller acceptance.

There was such beauty in the prayer, such belief, such obvious and transparent joy, that even the harshest, most cynical part of Albanus's mind began to question whether there might not be a great truth behind this faith. What if the priest tells me is right, and there is an almighty being who cares for each of us and will give us love, not fear, in return for our devotion? Is it too much to believe that love should be the strongest determiner of the world, and not hate? Or is that not just too simplistic, far too naive – a delusion for fools?

How the priest came and went from here – this small flat in a decaying block, surrounded by ordure and probably hidden, watching faces, any one of which might betray him – Albanus still did not know. As Icheka had told him, he was now clean-shaven, which made him, to Albanus's gaze, look shrewder and wiser and much older than he had done before with the bushy beard that had hidden half his face. He still wore his black cassock and hat at his services, but there was no sign now of his distinctive cape with its silver studs and high collar and dangling hood. I hope he does not put those on when he goes out, Albanus thought. It would identify his calling straightaway. There is even greater danger in what he does, owing to the Party's published proscription of the Christian faith that he had seen recently. The penalties listed were of the severest type.

Albanus continued to be worried about his own safety – at being seen and identified himself, which would mean most certainly the loss of his job and home, if not far worse. Nonetheless, he and Icheka continued to make their visits. As Albanus's faith gradually strengthened, he began to join in with the prayer, feeling belief and confidence growing within him, both from the prayer itself but also from the talks he had afterwards with the priest, whose pleasure at his slow but steady conversion was obvious.

'You now have a belief and a purpose, my son' he told him, enfolding him in his arms, 'something that is far greater than the daily call of survival. And your belief in God shall be a comfort to you, as he is with you at all times. When God calls upon you, you will be ready.'

A week or so later, Albanus learnt from the daily Party news sheet that came to his office that a few people 'calling themselves Christians' had been arrested at an outdoors 'ritual' they had been holding in a City park. They had been taken to the local police station and held there, until orders for their release had come from the State President himself; an 'act of extraordinary mercy', the report stated, as well as a warning against the practise of 'this vile religion', whose teachings 'threaten the stability of our new order, long fought for and thankfully now achieved.'

He wondered if these Christians in the report were of the priest's congregation, or some other. The news caused him much anxiety and, if he were truthful, fear as well. Perhaps someone, under intense questioning or even torture, would give his own description to the security police. He knew how increasingly vulnerable to discovery he was by continuing to embrace Christianity. He feared for Icheka also.

He wondered who the people were who had been arrested. Perhaps the priest had been among them? If so, would his release from any such confinement be on condition he disclose secrets of his congregation? Yet, he knew the priest would never betray his flock.

He had arranged with Icheka to go to Nanta's flat with her on the coming Saturday. He finished work at midday, and they met in the Party social club, as before. Icheka and he had replaced their work day uniforms with the common, grey Party boiler suits, hers no longer re-tailored but as shapeless as his own. The very drabness and conformity of this clothing seemed to afford them a type of invisibility among the ordinary people in the streets and flats, or so it felt, although Albanus realised how insecure was that delusion.

As they walked the streets together in the late afternoon on the way to the flat, he referred to the incident he had just read about. Icheka told him that by chance, on her way to the hospital, she had witnessed the Christian group being rounded up by the police, although she had not realised at the time who they were. The police had been very rough, she said. There had been only four of them, one was a young woman. She had fallen to the ground and been carried by the police to their van. Learning later from the radio, they 'were of the banned Christian sect'. Icheka prayed that this woman had been released with the others.

It had been a horrible sight to see, Icheka said. They must all be much more careful about where and how they worshipped in future. She had no idea who these Christians were, or where they had come from. Perhaps they had only recently arrived in the City and did not know the laws that prevailed there, or about the ever-watching presence of its large police force. They had probably left the City by now – perhaps a condition of their release.

Reaching Nanta's block, they climbed the by now familiar stairs to her flat. Once more they were fortunate, as they usually were, that there was no one about – no face looking out at them, no person on the landings or the stairs. It was very strange, Albanus thought, how seldom we meet anyone here. Yet, through windows, he could see the glare of screens, and sometimes hear voices raised, children screaming. If any inhabitant of these flats chose to report the repeated presence of strangers in the block, then it would be hard to find an excuse for what they were doing.

Albanus had to admit he was foolish in continuing to use this meeting place. Yet, where else was there? The priest had never suggested one. So the risk in using Nanta's flat was surely worth the taking. It was something far greater – far more powerful – than the Party to which he now wanted to dedicate himself. But Icheka? She shared the same risks as he. How could he protect her? Apart from being as cautious as possible, he did not know. All he could really do was trust to fate – or trust to God, if he accepted fully what the priest taught him. Then the good fortune that had accompanied him for so long might go on. But if it ran out, what would he do then? He had no answer.

Nanta opened the door of flat 2337 to their knocking. By now they had learnt the code of the faithful – three quick knocks, then two longer ones. Nanta was looking strained and tired. There were dark circles under her eyes.

'The priest is out,' she said. 'He wears his cassock and his cape. How can he be so foolish? I tell him, but he will not listen. God will protect us all, he says. We must have faith. I do have faith, but I worry too. We are hated out there.' She began to sob.

Albanus was shocked, not only by what she said but by the way she said it. It was unexpected. Nanta had always seemed so calm and assured. Were his worst fears suddenly to be confirmed? When he had last seen the priest, he had come to believe that he would disguise his vocation by wearing plain clothes when out in the streets, or at the very least move about by night only, although that might still be dangerous with the many police patrols about. Why then was he putting himself at such risk – wearing the distinctive cape again, for instance – and endangering the safety of his small flock too?

They went through to the lounge where the prayer meetings were held. 'Is anyone else due here this evening?' Albanus asked.

'Only one or two have said they will come,' Nanta answered. 'Our numbers are falling. The Party's new decrees have frightened them away.'

'What did the priest go out to do?' Icheka asked. She looked worried as well. Who would not be worried at this turn of events?

'He told me there was someone he had to find to bring back here. If all went well, he would not be long. Otherwise...' She flapped her hands helplessly.

'But why go out so openly!?' Albanus felt matters had got out of control. This was the situation he had feared. It was all going wrong. He had surrounded himself with foolish people with a hopeless dream. He had come to believe in something beyond his fear, but perhaps that dream had been foolish too.

There came more coded knocking on the outer door. Nanta flew from the lounge into the hallway hoping it would be the priest returning. But it was a married couple of the faithful arriving for the evening meeting. They looked as concerned as everyone else when they were told the news. A further knocking, and two men arrived – known to Nanta but not to Albanus. Nanta made hot drinks for those who wanted them, and they all waited in the lounge for the priest to return. One of the men got up and left. Albanus had seen him fiddling uncomfortably, unable to remain seated. He sensed the man's faith evaporating as the dangers he might be in became increasingly apparent. Albanus could not deny he shared similar feelings. He remained seated, however. He had Icheka to protect, and the others too, if the very worst happened.

A further sudden knocking, no code here but heavy thumps on the door, this time, made with a fist. The bell rang too, its sound clear in the inner room. They all looked at each other with fear on their faces. Nanta got up to go to the door. Albanus followed her. It would be a brief struggle. He would have no time at all, but he would go down fighting.

Nanta opened the door. The priest stood there.

'Have the faithful come? he asked.

'Several are here.' Nanta answered, hanging onto the door frame to prevent herself from falling. 'Oh, my priest – my father – where have you been?'

'Someone is with me,' he answered. Appearing from behind the priest's black shape was a woman's face – white, the blue eyes staring, her hair bundled up under a head scarf. The priest pushed her forward into the hallway. She walked with a limp. Albanus knew her at once. The blood raced into his face, astonished, unbelieving.

'I have brought our sister Janita to join us,' the priest exclaimed. 'Please make her welcome.'

10

The priest said a prayer to thank God for Janita's safe journey to them. He then blessed them all for their forbearance, and apologised for the worry he had caused.

'This was the only way,' he said in his sonorous voice. 'I was told about the young Christian woman who had been knocked to the ground by the police, and where she was in hiding now, and I went to fetch her to bring her to us. Her companions, whose faith was weak, had fled the City leaving her alone, but she had been hidden by one of our congregation, who had found her in the streets.'

'But why did you not disguise yourself, at least cover your cassock?' Albanus asked. His joy at Janita's coming to them was expressed by the kiss he had given her and the way she had clutched at his hand. 'Oh, Albanus, it is so good to see you again.' The tears had run in her eyes.

'I did not conceal my faith,' answered the priest, 'because I do not fear those who might challenge it, and because the time is coming when we must identify ourselves and make a stand for what we believe in. As it was, I received little but some curious stares, and there were even a few individuals who asked me to bless them, and praised me for showing myself so openly, another reason I feel my course to be the right one. It was a boost to their spirits, they told me, and renewed their hope that had been dying. I feel sure I have not brought danger to you and this house. Yet we must prepare for the evil that may come amongst us soon. We shall not be afraid then, for our faith is our strength and our purpose, to cast forth the light so that others may share it too. It is God's work that we do now.'

Albanus thought, that is all very well, but how is he so certain? Even if he is right and he hasn't brought danger to us this time, the next time it may well be the opposite. It is almost as if he is following an instruction written down for him. He even seems impatient for the trouble he speaks of to descend upon us. I do feel fear at what he says – I cannot prevent it – for myself and for Icheka, and now for Janita too.

The priest conducted a short service. Albanus took part as well, as he had now become used to doing, standing in prayer, repeating the priest's words, although he was still not sure sometimes of their meaning, his arms outstretched before him like the others. Icheka and Janita knelt together beside him, their heads lowered, Janita's blonde hair, loosened now, spread over her shoulders. He had seen Icheka give a surprised look when he had kissed Janita's cheek, but she seemed to understand the situation. They prayed like two sisters side by side.

After the service was over, Albanus went over to Janita, who looked both flushed with excitement and exhausted at the same time. She was eager to talk with him.

'My mother died not long after you went,' she told him. 'There was nothing left for me at the farm, so after some time had passed I decided to follow you and come to the City to find you. I travelled with some others who are also Christians. The police recognised us almost as soon as we entered the City, and they took us away and locked us up. They were rough with my brothers in Christ, but they did not harm me, although they had knocked me to the ground. When they released us, they told us we must leave the City and go home or they would not be so nice to us next time. The men left for the country straightaway, begging me to come with them. But I wanted to find you, and hid myself in back alleys, sleeping in an old shed and stealing food scraps from dustbins. I must have been seen, however, by someone who was sympathetic to us, for Father Amphibalus was told and came to find me and brought me away. Nanta, who is so kind, has said I can stay on here until I know better what I shall do.' She laughed, 'I must share a bed with her, however, as the priest has the other room.'

Suddenly, she broke down, sobbing into her hands. For the first time he realised her utter exhaustion, saw the twisted, bedraggled locks of her hair, the dirt on her skin and the grubbiness of her clothes. She had joined in the worship when she might have washed and eaten and slept.

'Venrig forbade me to leave him, but I disobeyed him. He is a brute these days and has turned to drink again. But he *is* my brother. Perhaps I have sinned in leaving him.'

So he did recover from my blows, Albanus thought. At least in his body, if not his mind. I am glad I didn't kill him that night. He took her hand. 'You did right. You have been strong. Far stronger than I. I believe I know the truth now.'

'The truth?' she queried, her eyes shining with her tears, looking up into his face. 'What truth do you speak of?'

'The truth of your Christ,' he answered. 'Who is *my* Christ now. For I do believe – yet it has taken me a long while to understand.'

'I am so happy for you, Albanus.' She raised a hand to touch his face and he kissed her fingers. 'But what is to come now? For you work for the Party, or so the priest has told me. And your friend here....?'

She looked across at Icheka, who came to her at once and embraced her. If there was any jealousy in Icheka, she certainly did not show it. 'You work for the Party as well, I think,' Janita said to her.

'I do,' she answered. 'Many of us *must* work for the Party or we starve. Yet in time we pray that the Party will come to accept our beliefs and even take them to themselves. Their rule would be a far better one if they only did so, for we do need strong leadership in these present times to rebuild our nation after so much war.'

This was quite a speech for her, which she delivered in a firm voice, standing before them determinedly. Albanus was impressed.

'It is yet a dream,' said the priest, overhearing and coming up to them, 'and a hope – a very strong hope that I know one day will come true, but for the present we are likely to receive their enmity, and increasingly so. We must take care in our worship and move as God will show us.'

And the priest talks now of care, thought Albanus. He that has just been so reckless and disregarding of danger. Yet, it seems he knows all that happens, and is to happen. He has that certainty about him – as he has always had since I first met him – which troubles me, as I do not understand from where it comes. Can it even be from God himself?

They had a meal of bread and smoked fish, which Nanta passed around on plates, and they eat with their fingers. Then the others present left, leaving only Albanus and Icheka. Janita had gone to lie down and rest.

The priest took Albanus to one side. 'My son,' he said. 'It is a joy to me to see how far you have progressed in God's love, and have come to accept him and his own son, Jesus Christ, into your life. Now I believe you are ready to receive God's spirit and enter fully into the church of Christ. I speak of your baptism.'

'Baptism?' Albanus answered. 'Why that? For I do believe now with all my soul, and I do not need a ceremony to tell me so.'

'Baptism, my son, is what the Lord himself taught us, as was performed for him by the holy saint John, he who is known as the Baptist. By the water of baptism you receive God's spirit and you are immersed in the faith of Christ. Without baptism, you cannot enter heaven, such is our belief, although I do think God in his mercy would not close heaven to those who have otherwise lived good lives. Yet for you, dear Albanus, it is necessary. When you are baptised into God's holy church you will be able to live with him, in mind and deed, in life and death, forever.'

'If you say it is necessary,' Albanus replied, 'then I would wish it. How, and where, will you do this for me?'

'I will let you know. There are some others I would wish to baptise also, but I do not know yet if they are ready to receive God's spirit, as I know you to be. There is a green meadow through which the river flows, beyond the Arena at the north of the town: that would be the place I would choose.'

But that is an open meadow and visible from the road, thought Albanus. I know it well. It would be dangerous. Party spies would easily see a gathering there and report it. We could all be arrested. And the priest has just talked of being careful. Why is he so contrary at times?

He asked: 'Could not baptism, which I understand must involve water, be carried out indoors, in a church, for instance? This country once had churches, I believe. I have read of them, and they had, I think, what are termed fonts at which baptism was carried out.'

'There is no church left in the City', the priest replied with a smile. 'They have all been destroyed.' His face is far more expressive now his beard has gone, Albanus thought, but he is still inscrutable.

'And I have no portable font,' the priest continued, 'or water that has been blessed, to carry out the ceremony in any other building. I need to use the river water – the water of life, as St. John himself called it – for I believe in the full immersion of the body, so that the spirit of God may be received fully and the soul cleansed.'

'But the danger at present...'

'Yes, the danger is a consideration. Of course it is, with matters as they are at present. And the time, as I have said, is not yet right. Yet, it will not be long. The time is coming. That's what I am told.'

'Who tells you?' Albanus asked, piqued once more by the priest's many mysteries, never explained, when so much could be at peril. 'Does God then speak directly to you?'

'Yes,' the priest answered straightaway, looking at Albanus directly, his eyes on his, his look very certain. 'Yes, it is God who speaks to me and through me.'

Albanus felt his own credulity wavering for a moment, yet he saw the calm assurance of the other, that what he spoke was true, and he *believed* him.

'And when is it that he speaks to you?' he asked.

'At all times, at any time, in the night-time, in the day: his voice comes to me as I sleep or as I walk out in the busy day, in the fields and in the streets'

I *do* believe him, Albanus determined again. Yet earlier I would just have said he was deluded, or even a little deranged, if he truly believes God's voice – his instructions – come to him in such a manner, priest or no. Yet, I cannot doubt it now. My belief in God has to encompass many things that are strange and beyond my own poor reasoning. It is likely that I shall never fully understand – not in this life, anyhow.

He took the priest's hand. 'Father, I will wait to hear from you,' he said.

11

Albanus re-immersed himself in his work for the Party, anxious to justify his promotion and to give a good account of himself to his supervisors, despite his inner turmoil concerning the Christian beliefs he had so unexpectedly – he had to admit that – come to accept. He felt that by so diligently performing the tasks he was allotted, he would be seen to be a thoroughly loyal and trusted Party servant, in whom any illegal or subversive activity could not possibly be suspected. Yet he remained fearful of being exposed as a Christian.

Had anyone, for instance, witnessed and reported him going to Nanta's flat? Were there Party spies watching him, gaining evidence against him day by day, whose reports might suddenly be acted on? He thought that unlikely, but he could not be sure. By burying himself in his work, he was able to forget his anxieties during the day. It was only in the evenings, by himself in his house, particularly during the long dark nights, that they emerged to trouble him.

There was no difficulty now in his seeing Icheka. Her occasional work for the State's prestigious Exterior Relations Department ensured she was a respectable person for any Party supervisor to be dating. So she visited his house often, attracting the glances of his spurned next-door neighbour, who would sometimes cast a spiteful eye over them as they came and went.

Strangely, they did not talk much to each other about their Christian faith. His forthcoming baptism, however, they did discuss, and Icheka – who too had yet to be baptised – seemed content to accept the priest's judgement that she was not yet ready for this, whereas Albanus was.

'Perhaps it is that I must atone more for my sinning,' she said, with a contriteness Albanus did not like. With or without baptism, he knew what a good Christian she had become. He was wary, in any event – even in his own home – of discussing anything the Party might think was subversive, just in case a listening device of some sort had been somehow inserted into the fabric of the house. Conversations that might be considered dangerous, he either had outdoors, or in a whisper beneath the bed clothes. It was not the way he wished to live, but for the moment he could see no alternative. Yet, why indeed should he be bugged, unless that was a condition inflicted on all Party employees of a certain seniority? As time went by, however, and no critical reports on him appeared, Albanus grew more confident that nothing was amiss.

A more Christian attitude to life, together with a fuller and deeper understanding of God's purpose for the world, did not mean Albanus and Icheka necessarily wished to live a chaste life. Neither the role of the monk or the nun appealed to them. Indeed, their sexual activity became more frequent. Albanus, in particular, felt a constant need for the release the sex provided from those inner tensions that still beset him. In response, Icheka was only too willing to please him.

After a particularly inventive piece of love making, she once asked: 'Did you ever do that with anyone else; with her, for instance?'

'With whom, my darling?'

'She with the limp, who you were so pleased to see.' It was not long after the priest had brought Janita to Nanta's.

'Janita, you mean. Don't be unkind, Icheka. She has had a terrible time. I have no idea what she will do now.'

'Didn't you...?'

'No, I didn't! Nothing like that.' He was annoyed. 'I felt sorry for her because of her lameness. It put men off her, she told me.'

'And you did not take advantage of that?'

'Of course not. It was a desperate time for all of us.'

He lied, of course. He *had* wanted to make love to her, and might well have done so but for....Memories of that dreadful evening when he had left the farm rushed back.

Shortly after this, Icheka received a message from Nanta at the hospital – a convenient and relatively safe place for communication – that 'she would like to meet her': this was their code that the priest wished to see Albanus again, presumably about his baptism.

The danger involved in going to Nanta's flat hung even heavier over Albanus now, but how else did he see his new faith continuing except by keeping in touch with the priest? He did not know the answer.

He seemed to be waiting on events, not trying to think too hard about anything but his work, yet feeling he was moving towards a situation beyond his immediate control – although unable yet to understand what that was or how it would be fulfilled. Events seemed to be speeding up towards some sort of culmination, and he began to fear what that might be. However, as the priest had spoken, he had been set on a path wished by God, and there was no escape. At times, when he was full of doubts, all this seemed to Albanus quite mad, and he prayed to God for understanding, and then his fears would diminish and he felt a sense of peace returning to him – only for the fears to start up all over again.

And he did fear greatly. At times, the terrors came upon him in the night, and he would awake, bathed in sweat, while Icheka would console him and try to calm him, so he could sleep again.

'I will be with you', she told him, 'whatever happens, to whatever end God calls us.'

When they walked to Nanta's flat after this latest summons, it was on an evening of dark, sweeping rain which acted as a good cover for them, for very few were about at all, and no one would have seen more than a couple of scurrying figures bent forward against the wind and rain.

At first, only the priest and Nanta were present, and then after some minutes Janita joined them in the lounge. She seemed to have recovered well, with a smile on her face, kissing both Albanus and Icheka, and hugging them to her.

'I have been with Nanta to the market,' she said. 'I had been frightened to go, as I felt so conspicuous by the way I walk. But no one seemed to notice. Few even looked at me. It is so good to be able to get out and about again. I am going to have a job at the market. A seller of fruit and vegetables, who is now growing too old to work by himself, said I could help him and he would pay me.'

'Be careful, Janita,' Albanus said. 'Do you really need the work?'

He turned to Nanta. 'I would help pay for her keep to make sure she's safe.'

'I need to have a purpose back in my life!' Janita cried out, looking distressed. 'I can't just stay here forever, doing nothing.'

'She will be all right at the market,' the priest said. 'I know the man. He is sympathetic to us, a Christian in thought and action, although he does not practise the faith He would not betray her and no one will suspect. The security police will have forgotten about her. It is I whom they seek.'

The last words made Albanus start. The priest had never talked before of any direct danger to himself.

'Yes, the time is coming,' said the priest. It was a phrase he had used several times before, and it brought a sudden dread into Albanus's heart. He took the priest to one side, almost pushing the bulky body in its enveloping black cassock out into the hallway.

'What do you mean exactly? Albanus asked. 'What time is coming and how does it affect me and you – all of us? Please tell now me in plain words, not metaphors or riddles.'

'As I have told you, a course has been determined for us by God,' the priest replied. 'I have known it for several years. I knew it was to be fulfilled when I first met you, and when I followed you, and when I lost you and you came to me again. And so we are here now, standing before God. His wishes – his purpose – must be fulfilled.'

'So you *are* still talking in mysteries, father.' Albanus was irritated again by the way the priest spoke. 'I hoped I'd made it clear and you would understand. I must have realities – not dreams – put before me, so I can prepare for them.'

'Ah,' said the priest, 'that is the crux – that is the cross indeed.' He would say no more, and Albanus was left more confused, and annoyed, than ever.

'What crux? What cross?' he asked.

'We shall see soon,' was all the priest would reply. 'And now I would ask you to pray with me, and with our sisters too, in the next room.'

They repeated his prayers, and even sang a short hymn about the Christ riding a donkey into Jerusalem through an arch of waving palms, for the time of Easter was approaching when Jesus was crucified.

'This is the most sacred time of all for a Christian,' the priest said, 'when the Son of Man gave up his life for us, and was resurrected, so that we who believe in him should have eternal life too.'

'Which of you believe in Christ, the Son of Man?' he asked his small congregation in turn. 'You, Icheka?'

'I do'.

'You, Nanta?

'I do'

'You, Janita?'

'I do'

'You Albanus?

'I do.' He repeated the words.

And I *do* believe, Albanus said to himself. I do not just say the words. So why am I now filled with more fear than I have felt for a long time? – more so than all those years of fighting, when I seemed much more reconciled to what might come, I mean my death, my extinction from this world. Perhaps the answer is that I had no hope then, and now I have the promise of Christ, whom the priest declares has a purpose for me. Is it then that purpose which I fear?

The priest told him: 'I wish to carry out your baptism, Albanus, on the Sunday of Easter when Christ rose from the dead. There will be three others of my congregations whom I will baptise too. One of those is you, Icheka, for I know you are ready now also.'

Icheka gave a cry of pleasure at this news, throwing up her arms and hugging Albanus.

The priest continued, 'The place will be the meadow I have already spoken of, beside the northern bridge, where there is a slipway into the river. The time, I propose, is at six hours when the sun is still rising and there will be few people about. Will you come to me there?'

'I will.' Albanus answered, as did Icheka. It was two weeks away. He knew he would be prepared by then.

'How good it is that we shall be baptised together,' Icheka said, taking Albanus's hand.

'I was baptised when a babe,' said Janita. 'I shall be present as well to see your joy.'

The storm outside was passing, and a last gleam of the setting sun, piercing the retreating cloud, struck on her directly, lighting her face and hair with gold.

Is this a sign she is one of God's chosen too? Albanus remembered thinking.

THE ARENA

Conversion and Sacrifice

12

At work the next day, Albanus received a surprise visit from one of his higher-graded supervisors, who gave him tickets for a football match to be held a week later in the City Arena. The tickets were a reward for him and his team for, what the supervisor termed, their 'excellent performance'.

'They are like gold dust,' the supervisor said. 'Every Party member wants one. So go off and enjoy the game. Mix in with your people a bit. The feedback I'm getting is that you're a bit severe with them. Give them a good time, and they'll work for you even better.'

The game was against Calpuchasia and expected to be closely fought. The winners would gain a gold cup to be presented by the State President himself. It was said the whole world would be watching on television. This was an opportunity for the State to give a better impression of itself beyond its borders. The progress that was being made – the development of the City, its new Presidential Palace, its law courts, its art gallery and museum, and above all its mighty Arena, long in construction – would be on show to the world for the first time. The world would take note. The world would be impressed. Very much depended, therefore, on this match.

Albanus did not enjoy football, nor did he like having to bend to his own team and treat them with familiarity. Most of them he disliked in their simple-minded worship of the Party, in their naivety, their coarseness and their vulgarity. Yet he felt he had no choice but to go to the match with them. He could not simply hand the tickets out and not attend himself. That would cause comment that might be harmful to him. He had to be appropriately enthusiastic for the sake of the Party. He was torn now between his responsibilities and his beliefs. What would the priest, or Janita, think of him? Icheka, of course, understood. She urged him to go and make a success of it. There was no ticket for her, however. He felt trapped, dreading the day of the match.

Everything, in fact, went much easier than he could have hoped for. The members of his team selected for tickets, ten in all, seven men and three women, were all dressed in their grey work uniforms, with Albanus at their head in his smartest supervisor jacket, stitched with his chevrons of rank.

From the offices, where they had all assembled, they took a tram to the Arena. There, they alighted to join the jostling crowds who were arriving from all directions. Channelled through a numbered entrance way, they reached their seats, which proved to be in a good position, low in the stands and at the front of their particular tier. Flags fluttered around the high oval of the walls above, and by the pitch Albanus could see the heavy television cameras being trundled into position. Television had been only recently re-introduced to the State, using out-dated equipment long discarded by neighbouring countries, after the destruction of much of its own infrastructure and communications technology during the long years of war.

Enormous cheers sounded out as the teams came onto the field. They kicked off. A referee in black darted about between the players, the State team in red and gold, the visitors in blue and white. A red and gold player was upended. Albanus found himself booing with the others, and then cheering like a mad man when the following free kick resulted in the ball flying into the top of the Calpuchasian net.

To many groans and shouts, turning into obscenities from some of those about him – but not from his own ten, he noted, with some relief, for he might be answerable for their behaviour in uniform if things got more out of hand – Calpuchasia equalled shortly afterwards. And so to half time.

The interval brought on a marching band from the State President's ceremonial guard, playing a strange medley of martial and popular music. Albanus was surprised to hear the latter, for much similar had been banned as degenerate by the Party when it seized power. Perhaps they were beginning to relax the more draconian aspects of their hold on society. Or perhaps they just wanted to give a better, more convivial impression to the watching outside world, showing a contented people united in all aspects of its culture.

Using his office's entertainment fund – a perilously small sum which he had to supplement from his own pocket – Albanus bought each of his ten workers an ice cream from a vendor who was hawking down the aisles. He watched them all sucking and licking contentedly at the dribbling ices, and thought it doesn't take much to keep the average worker – the average citizen – happy. But how deep was their satisfaction? Would they turn suddenly against him if they knew the truth about him? – he, a former fighter against the Party and now a Christian upstart, who sought to impose a kingdom of God upon them rather than a military autocracy.

He thought that not unlikely. They had been long conditioned to think one way only, and anyone and anything that parted from that view was an enemy. He might buy them ice creams today, but tomorrow they would bring him a rope to hang himself with.

The by now familiar stabs of fear started in his stomach once more, transferring themselves to his limbs and to his fingertips. What was he doing in this pretence? Why had he ever come here to enter into the service of the State, when he might have stayed largely free in the countryside, to wed with Janita perhaps and to live out his life honestly? He was caught up now in a subterfuge that might destroy him. Or was it a much greater cause he was following, as the priest told him?

He just wished things would come to a head soon and be clear to him – whatever the consequences.

In the second half, the State team scored again to rapturous applause, and then once more: 3-1 to the State. Calpuchasia was humbled, its players, as the final whistle was blown, left gasping on the ground. Albanus hoped they would not be punished by their own president across the border. It was only a game. His own team – and the crowd – were ecstatic. Albanus thought he should show he celebrated with them.

Outside the Arena, he pushed his way into a bar, the throng there standing aside when they saw his uniform, and bought beers for all his work team, which two of the women collected and took outside. They drank them standing together on the clipped grass of a park. These were *his* ten workers: he felt proud of them now. He had trained them, he had led them. And they had behaved just as he wished them to do.

He saw one of the men fussing at a girl, fingering her hair, stealing his hand into hers. Perhaps I should leave them, he thought. They want to enjoy themselves properly, and who am I to prevent them doing so? It's what I would have done once – but not now. I have too much weight on my shoulders, too much of a burden to carry. It's as if I am bearing the world on my back – of what has been and of what is to come.

But that is a fantastic idea, he reflected. Who am I to think that anything I do now or in the future will matter to anyone else? Only to Janita and Icheka, perhaps. They are all I have. And then the priest's face loomed suddenly into his inner vision, and he realised he was more than blessed. I have Christ now. He is always with me. I should not forget him during my business of the day. He will tell me my purpose, as the priest has said so mysteriously. I will know very soon.

He made his farewell to his ten, telling them to enjoy themselves but to remember their uniform and not to be late at the office in the morning. He had to say that; it was expected of him, although he realised he did not really care – and then he walked away.

Deeper into the park he went, where some couples, lying together on the ground thinking they could not be seen, and not really caring if they were, were already celebrating the day by the rhythmic fusion of their bodies.

He looked back towards the Arena. Its white walls were lit by the late afternoon sun, the coloured flags above streaming out in the breeze. As he watched, the sky seemed suddenly to darken as if thick cloud was obscuring the sun, yet he felt its heat still on his face, and the curving walls of the Arena changed colour; no longer were they white but now grey, with great, blackened posts set within them, and at one point a stairway rising against the wall, upon which he could see figures climbing and descending. The grass was no longer bright green, and he was standing as if on air, the ground below his feet hard and stony. There was a sound about him of cheering. He felt a sudden motion of being jostled and his body being seized by many hands, and he cried out in his fear and could not move, for it was as if he had frozen stiff. Then, as suddenly as it had come, the mistiness cleared and the white-walled Arena appeared again bathed bright in sunshine. He stood there, his limbs trembling, thinking what has happened to me? Am I ill?

Beside him, he saw a couple of lovers on the ground, raised up on their elbows, looking across at him with alarm on their faces.

'Go away, weirdo!' the man yelled, and made as if to get to his feet.

Albanus turned hurriedly and walked away, pleased to find his power of motion returned. He found an empty bench and sat on it, his hands still shaking. After a time, he recovered himself entirely and made his way home, where Icheka awaited him.

'What is wrong?' she asked, seeing he was troubled.

'I don't know,' he replied. 'It was as if I slipped into another time. Or perhaps I'm going mad – but I don't really think so. I simply can't understand what happened to me.'

He told her then what he had experienced, and now she was troubled. 'If this comes on again you must see a doctor.'

'I don't think it will,' he said. 'But if it does, I feel it will be something that is meant to be, something beyond my ordinary comprehension, if that makes any sense. I believe it might be a preparation.'

'A preparation for what?'

'I don't know. I can't tell you. But that word came into my head at the time.'

'You need to get some rest. You've been very stressed of late.' And Icheka insisted he go to bed, before she left in her Party car for her own lodgings near the hospital, where she had to be at work early the next morning.

When she had gone, Albanus found he could not sleep, or even lie still, and he got up and sat at a table in his small kitchen, watching the clock steadily ticking away the minutes and the hours, as if they were eating up his very life. He found himself thinking of his father, and of something which he had told him once about the ancient Rome he had lectured on at the university, something too perhaps about his own name Albanus, but he could not quite remember what it was. He was unlikely ever to know now. He fell into a sudden, deep sleep at the table, his chest and arms sprawled over it, until eventually the dawn light awoke him. Then he dressed and showered.

He felt strangely rested, alert and ready for this new day. He was at the office before any of his staff, and he had occasion to reprimand several for being late or for slackness with their work. Yesterday had never been. He preferred to forget it.

13

In the week before the Sunday of his baptism, Albanus refused to think of anything but his work for the Party, at his shiny new office with his by now well-trained team, all of whom seemed at least to respect him, if not necessarily like him. Again the thought came to him: how would they view me if they knew I consorted with Christians; indeed that I now declare myself *to be* a Christian? Why, he wondered, is the Party so hostile to Christianity? Why have they made such laws against its practice – and of other religions too, for that matter, yet Christianity above all.

In ancient times – and he did recall now something of what his father had told his brothers and himself – the Roman rulers had hated Christianity at first because its adherents refused to worship the emperor as a god, saying that their true God – their one and only God – had precedence in everything. This had led to much persecution of the Christians, and many had been put to death.

Did then the Party hate the Christians for much the same reason? – that they feared any allegiance to beliefs other than their own, feeling they might undermine the rule of their State. But would the Party then at some future time not come to accept Christianity, as the Romans had done, and draw strength and virtue from it, which should mean a better life for everyone? The later Roman emperors had ruled under the banner of Christ, and had spread Christianity far and wide as the one, true religion, even to this remote land on the eastern borders of their empire, which was their State today, now conquered and controlled by the Party.

Did he – Albanus, only as yet a low grade Party employee – truly believe that a Christian conversion would one day happen in this State too? That in time the Party would come to perceive Christianity as a strength, and not a threat?

If so, was that then the real reason for his own conversion, the purpose even of his coming baptism, that it was driven by a material ambition as much as spiritual? Should Christianity come to be accepted by the State to the general joy of its people, then his own role as an early convert, bravely defying the State's oppressive prohibitions, might be seen as remarkable and forward thinking – a hero to State and Party, rather than a dangerous subversive. Such a status would surely secure his rapid advancement and bring great material reward.

These absurdities he dismissed almost at once, angry with himself that he had even thought of them. He realised it was the devil putting the ideas into his mind – as the devil had tempted Jesu in the wilderness. No, it was something else entirely that was drawing him on – something far greater than mere personal ambition, something he had yet to understand fully and perhaps never would.

On the Sunday morning, he dressed himself with care, knowing that his body was to be immersed in the river without the encumbrance of clothes, as a babe from the womb to be reborn again. He wore a long, grey tunic – an item of clothing approved for off-duty wear by the Party – with just a pair of briefs beneath.

Icheka would be with him, of course: she had walked to his house from the City centre the evening before, and was beside him this morning, dressed similarly to him, her blonde head covered by a grey cap.

He had hoped Janita would be there as well, as she had said she would be. Yet, perversely, he now found he did not really like the idea of being exposed before her in this way. He did not know why. It was quite ridiculous, given the solemnity of the occasion and its meaning. Amongst Christians, he knew there should be no secrets, no inner vanities; the soul was to be clean and unsullied, without any shame or embarrassment of the body.

There is a depth to my feeling for her that may explain this, he mused. Then there came to him, unwanted and uncalled for, the lustful thought: naked to make love to her, not for her to see into my soul.

He dismissed this at once, feeling shocked and ashamed of himself. It was quite wrong, particularly on this morning of all mornings. He could not go to baptism with such base thoughts in his head. Should he not then defer the whole thing? For the moment, he felt unsettled, and it was only after kneeling in prayer that he was able to continue. Baptism would help wash away his sin, his prayer seemed to tell him. Yet, an echo remained in his mind: how could anything I would do with Janita ever be considered a sin?

Albanus, with Icheka beside him, had planned to walk to the place of baptism from their house. The meadow beyond the northern river bridge that the priest had specified for the service lay only a short mile away. They would set off as soon as it grew light enough to see. They should reach the meadow well before the six o'clock time the priest had specified.

And so that day, they walked out into the grey dawn, tiptoeing down the front path to the street, seeing a light on in the neighbour's window and hoping she was not looking out, their two grey shapes soon lost amongst the greater grey about them.

The daylight had begun to strengthen by the time they reached the main road. They followed the footpath at its side, with no one else about except the very occasional vehicle that was heading out of the City. It was Easter Sunday, when in the past the church bells would have been ringing and the good folk preparing to go in their best clothes to morning service. But that was no more. Now the State was atheist by decree. Yet strangely Sunday was still a day of rest. It tended to be used now for military parades or other Party celebrations, although nothing of that sort was due to happen this Sunday, as far as Albanus knew.

Nearing the river bridge, the road rose high on an embankment, below which at one side lay a straggling industrial estate, largely abandoned from the last period of economic prosperity before the war. On the other side, an open meadow of long, straggling grass stretched away beside the river, which made a wide curve here before winding away to the north. At the centre of the curve was a stone slipway where barges had once berthed. Now only a few thin cattle browsed the grass below the bridge's rusting iron piers.

Albanus looked down at the meadow from the embankment. There were still pools of darkness that the rising sun had yet to penetrate, and a white mist clung in places to the grass. There was no sign yet of the priest, or of the others coming to the baptism. He looked at his watch, which had been a present from his father and had miraculously survived the many perils of his life. The time was nearly fifteen minutes before six.

Taking Icheka by the hand, he was about to descend the concrete steps that led down to the meadow, when he heard the sound of footsteps approaching on the bridge carriageway.

He stood frozen, vulnerable, without possible explanation if this should prove a party of police or other officialdom. But coming over the crown of the bridge was the unmistakable shape of the priest, wearing his cassock and high collared cape and round, black hat.

Oh, why? oh, why? Albanus thought, could he not leave off those garments that rendered him so distinctive. He thought the priest had agreed to do so. Was he then courting disaster?

The priest was followed closely by the others with him – a man and a woman Albanus did not recognise, and behind them the lurching figure of Janita, whose face broke into a smile when she saw him before her with Icheka.

'It is well met,' said the priest loudly. 'Have you been waiting long?'

'No, but let's get below.' Albanus was impatient to be out of sight of the roadway, where a Party convoy might appear at any time. All his fears and doubts had returned. Was any of this wise? The priest once more seemed oblivious of danger – of his own safety or that of anyone else around him.

They descended the steps to the platform below the bridge. This was where he had brought Icheka before, Albanus remembered, trying to banish any feeling of shame at the memory, as his mind should now be settled and joyous. Did she recognise the place too? If so, she said nothing, but he felt a pressing of his hand, so perhaps she did.

Under the bridge, an earthen path led out into the meadow, which they followed, the priest in front. He must have been here before, Albanus thought. Has he performed other baptisms here? If so, when? Why is everything he does such a mystery? Perhaps when I am baptised, all will become much clearer to me.

Janita came to his side. 'Look,' she said, her eyes wide with wonder. 'See how the sun is rising in glory'.

And that did seem true. Yellow rays of light were flooding the meadow, striking away the last of the mist, which shimmered upwards in spirals like wisps of smoke. They are like men's souls was Albanus's thought: one minute here, then disappearing into nothingness.

He realised how pent up he was. This was meant to be an occasion of peace for him, but as yet it was one of worry.

In the shelter of the embankment that loomed above, Albanus had felt somewhat safer from prying eyes, but not when the priest struck out to cross the meadow towards the slipway. Now, they could be seen by anyone who cared to gaze down from the height above. Few places, he thought despairingly, could have been more public. For a forbidden rite to be carried out so openly, in full view of those who might report it, was surely madness – a danger not worth the taking.

What did the others think? He looked at their faces, but no one seemed to be concerned. Both Janita and Icheka appeared happy and relaxed as they walked beside him. The others showed no concern either. No one glanced about, as he did. They trusted the priest entirely. Seeing Janita stumbling beside him over the tussocks of grass, Albanus took her hand. He walked on between the two women, his strength renewed by their conjoined touch.

They halted at the slipway, where the river water washed over the far end of its cobbled, stone surface. Across the river amongst the thick reeds lining the far bank, Albanus could see some red-headed ducks drifting gently, one with a trail of its young behind.

The priest said to those gathered about him. 'You are about to enter into baptism, in which you will receive God's spirit, his love and his strength. With his spirit, you will not need worry about anything that seems at enmity with you, at this moment and forever after, for what you do now is to enter into the centre of everything, to be at the very core of your being, for the present and for all time, whatever shall happen to you. Remember that our Lord Jesus came to Jerusalem, where his enemies dwelt, quite openly, and he went to his death forgiving those enemies. Out of his strength we gain ours today for those things that must be done. And so, are you all now at peace?

'We are,' they replied.

Albanus felt the priest's words directed particularly to him, on account of the worries he had expressed. Icheka too had been fearful of being observed by outsiders during the baptism; they had discussed it more than once. But now she appeared calm, her lips parted in a smile, her eyes not leaving the priest.

'Janita,' the priest said, 'will you hold the clothes for us.'

He then motioned to the four of them to take off their shoes and to disrobe, and they entered the water behind the priest, who had hitched up his cassock in one hand, while holding out his wooden cross with the other. When the gently-flowing waters were up to his knees, he halted and motioned for the four to surround him.

Albanus's toes were curled into mud, standing at the very edge of the slipway. He could sense Icheka was worried about falling and he took her hand to steady her. The other man did the same for the woman, these two being totally naked. They are like Adam and Eve, Albanus thought.

'I call upon you to confirm you seek baptism into God's most holy house,' the priest intoned.

'We do,' they replied in unison.

'Then I baptise you in the name of the Father and of the Son and of the Holy Ghost.'

In turn, the priest took each of them into his arms and held them, bending his knees to allow the water to flow over the length of their bodies, then raising them again and making the sign of the cross upon their foreheads, saying, 'Through this water washed upon you, you receive God's spirit.' Albanus was last.

'Go now and live in Christ.'

They waded back up the slipway, laughing amongst themselves, their faces full of joy. Janita, smiling, handed out their clothing. They re-dressed themselves and bent to lace up shoes, while talking excitedly to each other.

The priest pulled down his cassock hem, re-slung the cross about his neck. 'And so it is done,' he said. He looked into Albanus's face. It was a look full of a meaning that Albanus did not understand.

They began to walk into the meadow from the slipway, Albanus holding Icheka's hand, the others behind. It was then that the voices began to call. Looking up, they saw faces – youths, it seemed – staring down at them from the bridge.

'We saw yer. Perverts.'

'Naked. Up each others' bums in the water.'

'Disgusting.'

'It's them Christians.' This from a woman who stood alongside the youths. She had short-cropped hair and wore a Party uniform.

The joy fell out of Albanus's soul when he saw her. So that which he had feared most had begun. And yet he was baptised, as he had wished, and he felt his belief to be strong.

He ignored the jeers raining down – as the others were clearly trying to do as well – and said to Icheka beside him. 'I love you'.

Then, turning to Janita, who walked with them: 'I love you too, Janita, for you were the first who taught me not to hate.'

She was to keep those words close to her for the rest of her life.

14

The taunts and obscenities were harder to endure once they had climbed the embankment steps and stood again on the roadway.

'Dirty pervs! Dirty pervs!' the youths chanted, surrounding them in the road but not coming close. One picked up a stone and threw it at them. Another did the same.

'You should all be arrested!' yelled the woman, picking up a handful of gravel and flinging it too. Some hit Albanus in the face, and he ducked away, pulling Janita and Icheka closer to him to protect them.

'Follow me,' the priest called out. He began walking fast towards the City end of the bridge, his cape with its hood billowing out, as the others hastened to catch up with him.

'Can you manage?' Albanus was concerned about Janita, whose limp made it hard for her to keep up.

'Don't worry about me. I'm all right.' Her breath came in gasps.

At the southern end of the bridge, the priest stopped. Their persecutors, Albanus was relieved to see, were not following. Instead, he saw the woman in the middle of the road. She had stopped a car and was pointing at them. Albanus knew this was more of a danger to them than the flung stones. The car driver might be able to summon the police – and quickly too.

Many Party officials, he knew, had phones in their cars for that very purpose.

'We must keep going,' the priest said. His chest was heaving. His air of calm authority, Albanus was alarmed to note, seemed for the moment to have vanished.

Above all Albanus's mixed emotions he was angry now – the peace and joy of his baptism so quickly upset, now this sudden threat that brought back his old fighting spirit, long in abeyance, with its shrill call for action. He was angry with the priest for having so endangered them, and he was angry with those who were deriding them.

Surely the baptism could have been carried out in another way. In that outrageous cape and the long, black ballooning cassock, the priest had stood out as clearly as the full moon in a black night sky –he must have realised that! Could it be – for a reason I cannot conceive of – that he is deliberately setting himself up for arrest, and we, his followers, too? What would be his purpose in that, this man I have come so to believe in? Does he want to destroy us all in some great sacrifice for the faith, in the belief that this is what God wishes also?

'Where then are you going?' Albanus yelled in the priest's ear.

'The Lord will show me the way,' he answered gruffly.

There was spittle on his lips; his dark face dripped with sweat. If I did not know him better, Albanus thought, I would think him scared, he who has never shown fear to me before, or any emotion really, other than certitude. Yet, he remembered, he had been angry too, that first time when I met him and he had shot at the dog scavenging by the headless child.

'You must come with me!' Albanus said.

The solution had occurred to him in a sudden flash of thought, as swift as light itself, and at once all his doubts vanished with the sudden realisation. This then was his purpose that the priest had spoken of. This was God's purpose for him. The priest had been waiting for him to accept it. Albanus understood everything now. The priest's real fear had been that he, Albanus, would not recognise that the time had come – but now he had in an immensity of revelation.

'The Lord tells me that you must follow me!' Albanus exclaimed, flinging his arms out wide. He knew he had been right when he saw how the priest's features relaxed, and his lips even formed the semblance of a smile.

'You are blessed, my son.'

Turning to the others, who were looking at him as if transfixed, Albanus said: 'I will stay here with the priest, but you all must go on together, where you will not be recognised once you are amongst the crowds in the City centre. Get back to your homes and pray there. That is how you should keep the faith for the present.'

Icheka protested: 'I want to stay with you.'

'No, Icheka, my love. Not now. Not at this time. Go to your own flat now. Yet I will be with you later and always.' And seeing Janita's tearful look. 'As I will be too with you, Janita. Help your sister in Christ now.'

He saw Janita reach out and take Icheka's hand. He knew Janita would understand what he had to do, almost as well as he did so himself: it was as if they were actors in a play and reading from the same script. Hearing shouts behind him, he turned and saw the youths and the woman, with some others from cars that had stopped, coming towards them, yelling out, and he knew there was a need for action.

'Go now, all of you!' He gestured up the road towards the City centre, and they moved away together at once, the two whose names he had never learnt looking back wonderingly.

'Father, we must be quick!' Albanus shouted in the priest's ear. 'We don't want to be caught by this crowd.'

He had seen there was a path to their right at the end of the bridge causeway, which led away from the road onto a strip of tree-covered land bordering the river. He had been here before in the various explorations he had made of this part of the City. He knew the area was used at night by vagrants who would come into the City to beg in the streets, often to be picked up and thrown into Party trucks, most never to return. No one knew what happened to them.

They hastened down the path and in amongst the trees, where indeed a few grimy, bearded faces watched them out of muddied sheets of newspaper. At the far end, they reached a side street that ran beside the river between warehouses and factory yards. Being a Sunday, no one was about, only a cat or two watching them from the top of a wall. On the far side of the last factory where the street ended, a railway bridge crossed the river. Here, Albanus was able to climb a low wire fence, help the priest over, and lead him onto the tracks, and so tread from sleeper to sleeper between the iron framework of the bridge to the far bank.

He knew now where he was. Emerging from the bridge, the railway line ran beside a new housing estate currently being built, the bulldozed earth filled with the half-built shells of brick houses, with roughly-laid concrete roads running between them. These were to be further Party houses for its various supervising classes, similar to the estate where Albanus's own house stood, a short distance further on.

There was no one on the building site, other than for a caretaker who emerged from a hut waving a stick and shouting at them. However, they were too far away to be caught by him, or even seen close up, and they escaped through a hedge and over a fence, emerging onto a street which joined with the main road. Now, it was only a matter of a few hundred yards until they came to the street leading to the estate where Albanus lived.

They passed first under the walls of the office block where he worked, surrounded by its carefully tended lawns, and Albanus was alarmed to see someone leaving the building whom he recognised, and who raised an arm to him as he hurried by. He did not respond, realising now it would be known for sure that it was he who was with the priest in his clearly identifiable cape. So all his efforts to get home without being recognised had been to little avail.

'Father, could you not at least take off your cape and hat and hide them in the hedge, so you are not so easily seen coming to my house?'

'Albanus,' he replied firmly, 'you will understand now that we both follow paths set for us to tread, as our Lord followed his to Calvary, and I would approach my Lord dressed as I was first attired in his faith, and which I have always worn during my ministry and will wear to the very end. I shall not hide from those who would persecute me.'

'Not even for my sake who will suffer with you?'

'Not even for you, my Albanus, for it is written so.'

Albanus did not argue further. He knew he could not alter the priest's mind, and yet there was an ending to be made of which perhaps even the priest did not know.

And so Albanus came into view of his house at last, he wearing his grey tunic, his flesh still damp from the river water, although perhaps it was his sweat now that ran on his body. Yet, where the priest had made the cross upon his forehead, the skin seemed to glow.

He hoped his neighbour would not be looking out as they came up to the front of the house. There was a way they might have approached from the rear, so as not so likely to be seen – a thick copse which came close to the house would have provided some cover – but he had not the will at present to suggest this, let alone action it.

He understood now that he had to accept the inevitability of his fate, although in what form exactly that might come he had as yet little idea. It would surely mean, however, the loss of everything he had so carefully striven for. He knew he was in the hands of God and must follow the path that was shown to him. That was what the priest had told him, and what he now understood. So, whatever was to come, it would be what he desired above all else. And yet this was harsh, very harsh, for any man – for any woman too – made of mere flesh and blood.

As Albanus pushed through the small gate into his front garden – it consisted of only a small patch of unmown grass crossed by a tiled path – he could see his neighbour's plump face peering around the half-drawn curtains, staring first at him and then, much more earnestly, at the strange form of the priest who followed him. It would not be long, he knew, before she was making calls to her superiors about what she had seen, who would more than likely report it on to higher echelons of the Party. She would enjoy her role in bringing down the man who had rejected her, this man whose clear involvement with the extreme Christian sect represented a danger to the Party and the State – and perhaps even to herself as well. What vile practices he might have plans to force upon her too!

It could only be a matter of a few hours – perhaps much less – and then the two of them – the priest and he – would be arrested; and to what punishment would they go? Albanus knew that any charge of subverting the State, if proven, could result in the death penalty. But for simply practising a banned religion? Did that carry a death sentence too? The Party might judge that to worship as a Christian *was* to subvert the state.

Once they were inside the house, Albanus ushered the priest into his small lounge, indicating he should be seated.

'Father, we need to talk; about how we are to manage things until the end that will inevitably come, for me, that is, for what I am – what I do – is known now, and no false stories I might give out will be able to deny this.'

The priest was wriggling out of his cape, which he threw into another chair, his hat upon it. 'Albanus, my son, it is not an ending that will come, but a beginning.'

'You are a master of words, father.' Albanus said this with a smile, whereas once he would have been irritated. 'I understand. I shall not be found wanting.'

The priest nodded. He seated himself.

'Would you take some food, father?'

'I would have a piece of bread.'

Albanus hurried off to his kitchen and brought back a plate with two roughly-cut slices of bread on it. 'Will you have something with the bread? Cheese, some potted meat, perhaps?'

'Not right now,' said the priest, raising his hand. 'Albanus, it would give me joy as your priest to give you communion.'

'What is communion, father? Is it with the bread and wine, as I have watched?'

'It is, my son. It is the meal Jesus took with his disciples before his arrest and crucifixion. The bread is his flesh, and the wine, his blood. By taking it into yourself you become one with the Lord, purified to be with him in his work, now and in the future.'

'Let me celebrate it then.'

'We have the bread, do you have the wine also?'

'I think I have. Yes, I am sure of it.' Albanus remembered he had bought a bottle of red wine at a City market the other week. It was made by a local vineyard, which since the war had managed to cultivate its grapes again. He bore the bottle into the lounge triumphantly.

'Excellent. Now, if you have two glasses.'

'Two?'

'Yes, Albanus, for I will be celebrating the communion as well.'

'So communion must be repeated?'

'Yes. As a reminder of Christ's sacrifice for us. A Christian's first communion is of particular importance, however, for through it, he or she enters for the first time into the kingdom of God, in company with all his saints.'

Seeing he was ready and standing before him, the priest rose and spoke the prayer:

'Almighty God,
to whom all hearts are open,
all desires known,
and from whom no secrets are hidden:
cleanse the thoughts of our hearts
by the inspiration of your Holy Spirit,
that we may perfectly love you,
and worthily magnify your holy name;
through Christ our Lord. Amen.'

Next, the priest read the Creed to Albanus, saying the affirmations of belief with him:

'Do you believe and trust in God the Father,
source of all being and life,
the one for whom we exist?

We believe and trust in him.

Do you believe and trust in God the Son,
who took our human nature, died for us and rose again?

We believe and trust in him.

Do you believe and trust in God the Holy Spirit,
who gives life to the people of God
and makes Christ known in the world?

We believe and trust in him.
This is the faith of the Church.
This is our faith.

We believe and trust in one God,
Father, Son and Holy Spirit.
Amen.'

And then the priest took the bread and crumbled it into pieces, while saying –

'He broke the bread, gave it to them and said: Take, eat; this is my body which is given for you; do this in remembrance of me.'

Both Albanus and the priest placed bread into their mouths. The priest continued –

'When supper was ended he took the cup of wine. He said: Drink this, all of you; this is my blood of the new covenant, which is shed for you and for many for the forgiveness of sins. Do this, as often as you drink it, in remembrance of me.'

Red wine was poured ruby rich into the crystal glasses. Albanus raised his glass and drank from it, watching the priest do the same. The priest's dark features broke into a smile.

'So, Albanus, you are truly of our Jesus Christ now. His body and soul are one with yours in this moment. Never forget this, however hard and fearful the road that is to come.'

They sat together in complete stillness for a while, a time of only a few minutes, but which Albanus felt to be a very long void of silence, as if he was suspended in a place somewhere completely free of weight and care, the light about him an orb of shimmering silver, within which he could see the myriad planets, and moons and vast, trailing clouds of stars in a firmament that revolved endlessly and forever, such colours too within it that he had never seen before, such distances his mind could scarce reach out to; and then he heard the priest's voice speaking out once more, and the vision was broken, dissolving and vanishing, and he saw the man opposite him in his black gown, with his eyes most earnestly upon him.

The priest, smiling, said, 'I think you are experiencing that peace which the true knowledge of Christ, and his love for you, will bring. You are blessed, Albanus. You are of the chosen, and I believe you are now in the presence of God our Father.'

Albanus replied, not knowing what else he could say. 'I do feel extraordinarily different. My worries and my fears have left me, and yet I know I should be frightened.'

'You are on the path now that has been made for you. The fear and the pain will return, but you have learnt what it is you must do and how it will be decided. You act with God . On the journey he has prepared for you, he will comfort you and strengthen you when you have the need.'

'Yes,' said Albanus, but feeling uncertainty once more, knowing his vision and the priest's words were all very well, and he did feel the truth of them, but reality faced him now, and how was that to be confronted?

Speaking slowly and deliberately, he said, 'I feel certain, father, that I will have been recognised. And you will have been seen too. Reports of the disturbance on the bridge will have reached those in authority. They will be looking for you also. You will have stood out clearly, so they will have your description, and others then will say they have seen you too; perhaps, I fear, at Nanta's flats, where they – the security police, that is – may come seeking you. And my neighbour, I am sure, even now is in touch with them, telling of what she has seen. The last is most unfortunate or we might have had more time.'

'More time for what?' the priest asked, looking at Albanus as if disapproving.

'So we might....' He wanted to say the word 'escape', and then realised he could not speak it. There was no escape. What was happening now had to be fulfilled. His own role in that fulfilment, he did not know yet for sure. Was it to stay with the priest, whose capture would be sought first and foremost? To protect him by force? Or...?

He caught his breath at his second, abrupt realisation that day. He, the soldier, who had been a man of action, a man who had risked his life time after time, was not needed now as a warrior, to fight and die on the battlefield. The sacrifice he must make – it was so suddenly clear to him – was to take the place of the priest, so that he could continue to do God's holy work here in this land of so much evil. The priest was one of God's messengers on earth, ordained to be a teacher of God's truth. He – Albanus – beside him was of little account. He could not teach, or travel the countryside with all its dangers, ministering to scattered congregations, as the priest had done, and would keep on doing if only he retained his freedom.

Albanus's purpose was now very clear to him: to give himself up to the Party – to the State security police –

disguised as the priest, thereby allowing him to get away. By the time the police realised their mistake, the priest should have reached safety, somewhere where he could begin again his holy ministry. He – Albanus – would be the victim in his place, the sacrifice that had to be made.

Albanus looked at the priest sitting so still and calm in the chair opposite him. 'You have known, haven't you?' he said. 'You have always known what would be required of me.'

'It is true,' he said, rising to his feet. He embraced Albanus. 'The purpose was told to me many years ago: that one day I should meet such a man as you – a man who had been a soldier – and you would become my champion against the anti-Christ.'

'Which is why you have always been so certain of me,' Albanus said, the realisations once more exploding like stars in his head. 'And why you have had little care of late for your own safety, for you knew'... he tried to say the next words with no bitterness but nonetheless his tone betrayed him ...'that I was there to take the dangers from you.'

'It was never like that,' the priest said softly. 'For myself personally, of course not. But for our God, that he should be better known in this dark land of disbelief where evil rules, then, yes, that is true. Yet, I tell you, Albanus, you will be the blessed one – a martyr whose name will be remembered, not I, Amphibalus, and that is as it should be.'

Both sat in thought for a while. Then the priest asked suddenly, surprising Albanus by the question: 'I would be interested to learn your father's first name.'

'Sartor. My mother called him that, and the friends he had from the university.'

'Sartor!' For once the priest seemed surprised beyond the calm surety he usually showed.

'Yes. Do you find the name strange?'

'No, of course not. Yet it is not a common one.' The priest lapsed into thought. 'I had my suspicions by something a man said to me.'

'Which man?' Albanus was impatient now. 'What was said?' This was a distraction surely from the crisis they should be preparing to meet.

'The name Sartor is used by the fruit seller at the market whom Janita has begun to work for. He told me once he had worked at the university and fallen on hard times. He said he had lost all his family; that one son had gone off to fight, and he had not heard of him since.'

Now here was information to shake Albanus, quite wiping out for the moment all other matters. 'What age is that man?'

'He's old. It's because he's old that he now needs help with his stall.'

'What does he look like? Have you seen him?'

'Yes. He is a Christian, one of my flock, indeed, although he does not attend our prayers.'

'So he could not be my father.'

'Why not, my son?'

'My father was not a Christian. I do not know what his religion was, but he was likely an atheist, as I used to be.'

'He may have changed.'

Yes, thought Albanus. As I have done. 'What does this Sartor look like?'

'He has a round face, much wrinkled about the eyes and mouth. And white hair which he sweeps back. And he has lost the end of a finger, on his left hand, if I recall correctly.'

'That is him then!' exclaimed Albanus. 'He injured that finger when I was a boy. By all that is wonderful, he is alive. It is a miracle!' Thrills of joy filled him. He stood, his arms held out wide.

'It shows God's love for you, my son. You should thank him.'

'I will. I will.' And Albanus fell to his knees, his hands pressed together.

'I must go to him,' he said, still on his knees.

'Albanus,' the priest said sombrely, 'that will be impossible now, but I shall do what I can to see you look upon his face again.'

Albanus had changed his damp tunic for a lengthier one, brown in colour, and worn now with breeches beneath, and the priest had given him his huge encircling cape, with its metal studding set in the leather. When the time came, Albanus would put on the cape and pull up its hood about his face, so that from a distance he would be taken for the priest. The cape, with its bulging shape about the shoulders, would mark him out clearly to those who sought him. Albanus's height and profile in his dark tunic and cape would be similar to the priest's. Once his fair skin and hair was hidden by the hood, the disguise was complete.

Albanus felt sure the police would be seeking for the priest before they came for him. They knew where he lived, anyhow, and could find him at any time – unless he too made a run for it. No, undoubtedly, it was the priest they would look for first, knowing now he moved about the City and wanting to catch him before he got out into the suburbs and beyond. But when they found him, as they inevitably would and quickly too, it would be Albanus instead they had in their grasp. In the meantime, most hopefully the priest would have made his escape.

The priest had agreed to this plan eagerly. No longer did he speak of retaining his own priestly guise at all costs, for now the circumstances were different. It was Albanus who would be using it for this one, vital purpose. Perhaps what was to happen now had been the priest's own intention from the very beginning.

The priest retained his cassock and breeches, but lifted the hem of the cassock to pin it up around his thighs so that it looked more like one of the State-approved tunics still worn by older citizens during the day instead of a boiler suit. A pair of Albanus's long socks covered his lower legs and over his upper body he draped a woollen mantle that Albanus had found for him, together with a canvas pack in which to carry his few belongings. Into this he had stuffed a piece of cold meat from the kitchen and a flask of water.

His look was a little strange, but many of the unemployed about the City, wearing bits and pieces of old clothing they had picked up or stolen, looked stranger still. It should suffice for him to have a good chance of escape. As regards his dark skin, there were many others of similar complexion in the City and the suburbs beyond, with whom he could hope to merge without undue notice. His first aim would be to get out of the City by following the northern road, the same road that passed close to Albanus's house.

The priest would exit the house at the rear, hopefully unseen by the neighbour, who was likely to be still watching the front path. From the kitchen window, he could see the dark green coniferous trees of the copse growing close to the back of the house, within which he could be quickly hidden. There was only a short space to cross before he reached it. Beyond the copse, he would come to another part of the housing estate entirely, one yet to be developed and unlikely to be watched, so he should be able to reach the main road without being observed. After that he must trust to God and his own wits.

Once he knew he was safely away, Albanus in his disguise would leave by the front door, then maintain the pretence of being the priest for as long as he could, perhaps even after his inevitable arrest. He knew that timing and luck were vital. If the priest was seen leaving at the rear, then all would be lost.

And what if there came a sudden thudding at the door now – at this very moment!?

Despite this fear, however, the priest was intent on one last conversation with Albanus – the soldier he had converted and baptised as a Christian, who was now prepared to surrender his own freedom for him, and, if needs be, his life too.

'I would wish you to have this, my son,' he said, handing him the wooden cross which had always hung at his chest. It was on a loop of cord, which the priest pulled over Albanus's head. The cross fell down beneath the cape and was hidden.

'I am honoured, sir,' Albanus said.

'No, my son, The honour is to God, for whom you act now. Let us pray.'

He spoke:

'Our Father, who art in heaven,
Hallowed be Thy name,
Thy kingdom come,
Thy will be done on earth as it is in heaven,
Give us this day our daily bread and forgive us our trespasses,
As we forgive them that trespass against us,
And lead us not into temptation but deliver us from evil,
For Thine is the kingdom,
The power and the glory,
For ever and ever.
Amen. Amen. Amen'

'Now is the time. God go with you, Albanus.'
'And with you too, father, my dearest friend!'

15

Albanus quickly checked the front and rear of the house from his upper windows. He could see nothing suspicious. Certainly there was no one between the house and the copse, and no sign of his neighbour peering from her back windows, although he could not be sure of that. He ran downstairs, feeling heavy and awkward in the cape, the cross bumping at his chest. The priest was in the kitchen by the back door, his pack slung over his shoulder.

'Go now!' Albanus said, pulling open the door.

The priest left at once, not turning his head. Albanus watched him crossing the strip of open land, and then he was in amongst the trees and out of sight. It happened so quickly that for a moment Albanus stood as if stunned, thinking this is not real. Are these things truly happening to me, or am I in a dream?

Then, gathering himself, he raced upstairs to look from the front windows. He squinted through a gap in the blinds. There was some movement in the street. A family group walked out, small children holding their parents' hands, a boy and a girl excited by the prospect of a day without lessons. Perhaps they were going to the amusement park beyond the river bridge, where there were helter skelters and dodgem cars for the children of Party members. Few of those of his

Party rank who lived here had motor cars, but he did see a number of vehicles – two cars, a lorry and a van – passing the house. One car stopped further down the road. Was someone watching from it?

He had to take a chance. The longer he waited before leaving, the more likely it would be that they would come to arrest him at, or near, his house. He wanted to get as far into the City as possible before he was caught and forced to reveal his identity, giving more time for the priest to make his escape.

The sky that had been so bright at dawn, he saw now had darkened, and a thin rain was already misting the air. That was good. It would make his wearing of the cape look more natural than on a warm day of sun.

Back down the stairs to the front door he ran. He took a deep breath, taking a last look at his house. He pulled up his hood. Then he opened the door and stood outside – exposed!

Was his neighbour watching, even now reaching for the phone to tell them that he – the priest – was leaving? He is wearing a strange cape, very distinctive: it is decorated with metal studs, she would be saying. Or would she have recognised him despite the cape and the hood. Would she see the white skin of his hands? He pushed them up into the cuffs of his tunic sleeves, and started walking, out of his front gate and onto the street. No one came to him from the parked car. Its driver seemed intent on his passenger, whatever it was they were doing together.

Albanus passed the office block where he had worked and came to the main road beyond. He did not turn to look behind him. At every step he expected to feel a hand on his shoulder, a voice calling out 'Stop!'

Before him on the road there was much traffic. It was late morning, and many people were out and about despite the spattering of the rain, which was not enough to drive them indoors. Some stared at him, clearly thinking his appearance unusual with the heavy cape about his shoulders and chest, his face buried in his hood, but none sought to stop him. A passing car sounded its horn, but to what purpose Albanus did not know.

He came to the bridge and crossed over it, looking out at the river and the meadow of his baptism, where he had been so joyful such a short time before. So much seemed to have happened, so much changed, in just a few hours, that it was as if he was in some other place and at another time entirely.

He walked on, coming into the much busier streets at the heart of the City. If they did not come for him now, how long would he go on walking? He sensed his plan already beginning to crumble. But, as long as the priest had got away, it did not seem to matter. Or had he already been captured?

Then, as had happened before, his vision suddenly began to break up and be lost in mist to re-emerge as something else entirely. He staggered and stumbled, and nearly fell.

Someone called out: 'That man is sick. Help him.'

He stood in a paved street and there were people around him. All he could see of them at first was a mass of coloured cloaks and flaxen-white tunics, some striped in reds and browns. Then a woman came up close to him; her hair was piled up in an elaborate coil, gold rings dangling from her ears. Behind her, he made out horse riders approaching, one of whom wore a silver breastplate and had a crimson crest upon his helmet. He clung to a wooden balustrade beside him, his head spinning. Then the view blurred and reformed and he saw the City street once more, the tall buildings lining it, and the people in their boiler suits standing about him.

'Are you ill, sir?' said a voice in his ear.

'Step back!' another voice called out behind him, one with authority. Albanus turned and saw it was a policeman in the

Party's grey-green uniform. He carried a pistol in one hand. A man in a plain grey suit stood with him.

'Are you Amphibalus, a Christian priest?' this man asked, looking into his face. He wore glasses with thin, gold frames. He will see my skin colour, Albanus thought. Yet there was no reaction.

'So you know my name', he answered. 'I am indeed Amphibalus. What do you wish of me?'

'I must take you into custody. Those are my orders.' He was perfectly polite, almost apologetic.

'Then I must come with you.'

Albanus was thinking, the priest will likely be well away from the City by now. They cannot then know he is dark-skinned and I take his place.

'Where do we go?' he asked.

'Just a short drive to police headquarters.'

Albanus saw the uniformed officer signalling to a police van to pull up at the kerb. 'Back! Back!' the policeman shouted at the crowd, which was growing bigger now, pressing forward to see what was going on.

The van doors were opened. The policeman pulled him forward by the arm. As he sought to climb the step to get in, he was pushed from behind. He stumbled, falling on his knees inside. In so doing, his cape was torn open at the front. The priest's wooden cross about his neck swung free.

'There's no doubt about you then,' the policeman said.

Nothing further was said to him as the van drove through the City. Albanus sat on one side on a metal bench with the uniformed policeman beside him, a hand fastened on his arm. The second of his captors – the plain-clothes one – was seated opposite. Both watched him intently. After some ten minutes, judging by the engine noise, the van began to slow down. Albanus could feel it turning sharply, and heard it clattering over a metal ramp. It stopped. All was still. Then the rear doors were flung open.

'Out! Out!' A snarling face was thrust into the van. He was pushed again from behind, so for the second time he fell down onto his hands and knees, his tunic rucked up. He had fallen onto concrete. Struggling to raise himself, he saw his knees were bleeding.

'Get that f---ing hood off your head!'

The hood was ripped back by this new grey-green policeman, who wore a broad leather belt at his waist and a narrower one diagonally across his chest. Inverted white chevrons decorated his upper arms and silver crowns his epaulettes. A black pistol in its holder sat snugly at his hip.

There was a pause while Albanus was examined intently, the policeman walking around him, then consulting a piece of paper he held.

'Who are you?'

'I am Amphibalus. I am a priest of the Christian faith'.

'You're f---ing well not. It says here you have black skin. *Your* f---ing face...' – he placed his own close to Albanus's – is f---ing white and f---ing red. You been out in the sun, f---head?'

'Yes. I burn easily.'

'Oh, you do, do you? A f---ing comedian too. Now, who the hell *are you*?'

Albanus did not answer.

The policeman, pink patches beginning to spread on his sallow cheeks, turned to the two captors, who were standing by, looking increasingly worried. 'You've got the wrong f---ing man.'

'But he matches the description, sir. We identified him from his cape.'

'He's obviously switched it with the man we want. Why didn't you take down his hood and see his face?'

'We weren't told he was black, sir,' the uniformed captor said defensively. 'We had no such information. Just the dress: a cassock and a cape.'

'And is this a cassock?' The policeman tugged at the hem of Albanus's tunic, causing him to stumble forward. He groped higher. 'It's just a tunic, a bloody tunic, and pants too He's fooled you.'

'Who the f--- are you?!' This was screamed inches from Albanus's face, followed by a blow across his mouth and nose with the back of a gloved hand.

Albanus knew he must not retaliate. He felt blood running from his nose and tried to wipe it away with his fingers.

Taking off his gold-rimmed glasses and wiping his eyes with the back of his hand, the plain-clothes captor now motioned the police commander to one side. They stood talking for a minute or so. He knows now who I am, Albanus thought. He has likely been watching my house and perhaps has even followed me to see where I went and what contacts I would make. He was fooled by my disguise, though. And no one could have been watching the back of the house. The priest must have got clear, or they would already have known about our switch.

The commander returned and stood before him. His face was set grimly. The pink patches had left his cheeks. He looks calmer now, Albanus thought, yet even more deadly.

'You are Kurt Detrichen, also known as Albanus – a Party member and a supervisor at the State Procurement Department?' he said in an icy voice. It was a statement more than a question.

Albanus knew there was no point now in denying it. I would likely be beaten further if I do. The priest is beyond any further help I can give him. He is in God's hands now, as I am too.

He said quietly: 'I am he. I am Albanus Detrichen. Kurt was but a name I used to join the Party.'

'So you are a liar too?'

'Only when I seek to protect the truth.'

The commander gave him a long, contemptuous look, then turned on his heel.

Two policemen seized Albanus roughly by the arms and led him away.

16

Albanus was left in a bare-walled cell for what seemed to him a very long time, but which perhaps was no more than a couple of hours. There was no chair to sit on, indeed the cell was bare of anything except a single metal pot, which he could see had been used by someone else before him and not emptied. It smelt. He pushed it with his foot further into a corner and sat down on the floor in the opposite corner, his back against the rough concrete wall. They had searched him and taken away his watch and the priest's cape, as well as the cross about his neck. The loss of the last, he regretted most of all, for the priest had entrusted it to him especially. Yet, he knew its taking was inevitable.

They had robbed him of his shoes too. In only his breeches and the cotton tunic, he felt chilled. There was no window to the cell, just a barred opening, no more than a foot square, high on one wall. It did not seem to admit light, and was probably just an air vent. The only light, in fact, came from a single bulb hanging by a short wire from the concrete ceiling.

When, with a jangle of keys and a crash of the lock, the cell door at last was opened Albanus had dozed off into a fitful sleep. Awakened by the noise, he tried to scramble to his feet, but the sharp pain in his knees meant he had to fall back against a wall for support. Quickly, he pulled himself upright.

Commonsense told him it was not a good idea to linger on the ground when men, adjudged your enemy, were standing above you wearing heavy boots. These were two prison guards, indeed jackbooted for their trade, wearing close-fitting black boiler suits and round shiny helmets.

They did not say anything, but pulled his arms behind his back and fixed them there with plastic cuffs about his wrists. One held the cell door open while the other pushed him out.

'Where are we going?' There was no reply. Albanus knew it had been silly to ask.

They passed down a corridor lined with other cells, and came to an open area where there were lifts. Others passed them, all these in the tailored grey boiler suits of State employees. Not one, Albanus noted, even cast a glance at him. In a lift now, they rose rapidly through several floors, then stopped as a white light flashed on the control board. With hands firmly on his bound arms, Albanus was led out by his guards and down a long bare-walled corridor until they stopped at a plain brown door at the far end. One of the guards knocked on it with his fist: it was opened straightaway. Albanus was pushed abruptly forward over the threshold. The guards disappeared. The door closed.

Albanus found himself staring at a row of four men and one woman, all in Party uniforms with differing badges of position and rank embroidered on their jackets. They sat, spaced out equally, behind a long desk made of pale yellow wood. A carafe of water stood beside each panel member, together with a large pad of white, lined paper. Files in red, yellow and blue covers were scattered across the desk top. There was no chair for him to sit on.

The room was brightly lit by banks of strip lights overhead. One long window beyond the desk was closed by the grey-green slats of a blind. On a side wall hung a huge, coloured photograph of the State President, wearing a white uniform jacket, highly emblazoned with multiple medal rows, crested silver buttons and coils of golden braid, with a blood-red sash running diagonally across his chest. Images of this all-conquering, all powerful individual were normally given out to his people to show him in combat uniform, perhaps emerging from a tank turret, or as a 'man of the people' wearing peasant's clothing, his feet planted firmly on some grassy hilltop, his head raised to gaze steadfastly towards the endless horizons of his destiny.

'Albanus Detrichen', said the man at the centre of the desk – he has a flat face, with a pug-like nose, as if someone has sat on it at some time was Albanus's thought – 'Would you confirm that is your name?'

'It is'.

'Albanus Detrichen. You have been arrested for involvement in the promotion of the preposterous, false and dangerous creeds and practices of superstition that are known as Christian, or Christianity, or God, Jesus, Christ, or Saviour, or whatever else of several other forms is currently the vogue in the practice of this delusion, it being contrary to the decrees, values and welfare of our State, as has been set down in law and outwardly declared by our President several times during the past year.'

He paused, while wiping his lips with a white handkerchief. 'My purpose as Chairman of this Panel of Inquiry assembled here is to gain an understanding of why you, a State and Party employee, of some merit according to your official record, who has risen to a position of responsibility, should have so betrayed the public cause that you are sworn to uphold. I am not here myself to judge you – that will come later – but I and my panel have been asked to make a preliminary enquiry about you and the circumstances of your betrayal.

Our report will be sent to the Office of the State President, for I am allowed to tell you that the President, himself, has taken a personal interest in this matter.'

'I am at your service,' said Albanus, as calmly as he could, although his heart was thumping.

'Silence!' the female panel member spat out. She had a narrow face with black eyebrows and reddened lips. 'You may only speak when you are directly asked a question.'

'My apologies'.

He felt sick, His whole body seemed to be trembling. He hoped it did not show outwardly. He wished he could be seated. Was he about to have one of those turns he had experienced recently, when he had seemed to be in some other place at some other time. What caused those? Was it stress perhaps? Or a brain tumour about to burst?

The last would certainly provide a quick way out of this! What he didn't want was to be degraded, to become irrational, to fall down and foul himself, or, worse, to beg for mercy. He wanted to show no fear at all. He was a Christian now, but he was a soldier too. He would always be a soldier – a Christian soldier. Was there indeed such a thing? The priest had certainly thought so. The priest! Why had they not mentioned yet the fact that he had been disguised as the priest? To them, surely, this must appear as his greatest crime of all, one with the intention of deceiving the forces of the State.

Was Amphibalus secure by now in some place of sanctuary? And Janita and Icheka: were they safe too? He thought of Janita in particular, and her odd, impeded, yet so determined walk, and the beauty he saw in her, and the love she had spoken to him, and he felt so sad that he was never likely to see her again. And Icheka, of course. Without Icheka, he would never have re-found the priest. He owed Icheka everything, and he told himself he loved her equally with

Janita, but he knew that his love for Janita was the greater. And now, did any of that matter? It was his love of God he must keep before him above all.

Albanus's reverie was broken by a sudden reference in the court room to the priest, just as he had anticipated. Despite its inevitability, it still shook him. The Chairman had been ranting on further about the evils that the 'cult of Christianity' could bring to the State, with absurd and hideous references to cannibalism and sexual perversions – 'well attested', the President declared – that were encouraged by those who spread the evil gospel of Christianity, men known as priests. And there was one such priest now in their City, he declared, whom the State security service had identified and been about to arrest when this man' – he raised his head to stare at Albanus while jabbing a finger at him – 'helped him to escape by *disguising himself in his own garments*'.

He emphasised these last words in a type of screech that caused the other panel members to join in, jabbing their own fingers at Albanus and hissing out, 'Shame'. 'Shame.' 'Traitor. 'Traitor'.

Some impartial examination this, thought Albanus, strangely feeling much calmer now that the role of the priest had been announced, and in such a ridiculous, obscene manner. The priest was central to everything he desired and understood. He had brought Albanus to Christ and had baptised him with his own hand. More than that, he had brought back Christianity to the City, where he had formed a community of Christians – a community that could hope one day to drive out the evil induced by the Party.

The Chairman now opened up his inquiry to the questioning of Albanus by individual panel members. The sharp-faced woman was first: she seemed to want to concentrate on the sexual perversion issue, as already outlined by the Chairman.

'Were you in receipt of favours from the priest, Amphibalus?' she asked, her hands placed together, fingertips to fingertips.

'What sort of favours, madam? Albanus asked.

'You know what I mean – of the body, of the flesh.'

'Only the bread and the wine, madam, which forms part of the service of communion.'

'And nothing sexual?'

'That is ridiculous, madam. Of course not.'

She looked down at some notes before her. 'It is said that lesbianism and sodomy are practised amongst the congregations of Christians, and that men also have women in common.'

Albanus laughed. 'That is nonsense put about by the devil. Christianity is a religion of love.'

'Exactly,' a male panel member spoke. 'Love is sex.'

'Not in our congregation,' Albanus said. 'I assure you we seek the purity of truth, nothing else.'

'But you then admit you are of a congregation of this proscribed religion?' the Chairman intervened.

Albanus felt a moment of irritation. He had been led into revealing himself, yet it made no difference. The fact was obvious, and he would have said so directly himself, anyhow. For the moment, however, he did not answer.

'And you could name your other – what shall we call them – worshippers?'

Again, Albanus did not reply.

'Silence is no defence,' said the Chairman.

'I thought this was an inquiry, not a trial.'

'It is. It is. We seek knowledge of all aspects of these matters, including any names you can give us.'

'I shall give you no names,' said Albanus determinedly. He set his legs apart and stood four-square to them, making his back as straight as he could, as if on parade. He was not intimidated by them now. He was certainly not frightened of them.

'We shall see about that,' said the Chairman with a sneer. 'This hearing is suspended at this point. We shall resume tomorrow.'

He pressed at a bell push beside him. It made a sharp, clanging sound in the room. The outer door opened and the jackbooted guards returned. He was escorted back to his cell.

They gave him a rubber beaker of water after an hour or so and a hunk of dry, mouldy bread, on a plate also made of rubber. If they brought china or plastic or metal into this cell, he realised, I might break it to make an edge to slice my veins with. He could only eat the bread by chewing it with the water in his mouth. I shall not be growing fat on this diet, he thought.

He lay down full length on the concrete floor, twisting onto his side to cushion his head with his arm, and he slept. He dreamed of angels that would come on powerful wings to rescue him, but, even in his dreams, he realised such hopes were in vain. His destiny lay elsewhere, as the priest had indicated. But what had it been that the priest had told him of?

He was not sure in his fuddled sleep, but that did not seem to matter. He knew God was with him: he knew that with a crystal-clear certainty – today, tomorrow, always.

17

They came for him again the next morning. He did not know it was morning, for there was no natural light in his cell and the electric light had been left on all night. He had been awake for some time before the cell door was suddenly opened with a crash of its bolts, and two of the uniformed gaolers stood over him as he lay on the floor. One of them nudged him with his boot. 'Get on your feet!'

He struggled to raise himself, but his body felt very sore, and he had to support himself again against the wall while doing so. 'We're going to make you prettier,' a guard sneered at him.

They took him bare-footed down a corridor and into a small room, which proved to be a wash room with a shower in the corner and a wash basin. 'Take off your clothes and leave them on the floor. We have some new ones for you.'

One of the guards remained by the door as he stripped and stood under the shower. The water jets were strong and the water hot. The cell door was opened and a female guard came in. She put down a pile of clothing and left with a backward grin. Albanus, still under the shower, did not try to turn away or shield his nakedness: he felt none of the indignity and embarrassment that perhaps were intended. He was beyond any concern of the flesh. He relished, though, the cleansing water, remembering the last time he had felt its power was at his river baptism, when the priest had held him in those precious moments, fully submerged. His weaknesses once more were being washed away.

He was allowed to shave. A safety razor, very blunt, was handed to him and a small cake of soap. Then he pulled on the fresh clothes – baggy underpants made of sacking, or so they seemed, and a plain, biscuit-coloured tunic of good wool, much warmer than the one he had been wearing when captured. It was long, well below his knees. His shoes were also returned to him.

He was then taken into another room, where at a table he was given food and drink – a roll of bread filled with some substance like cold sausage meat and a mug of lukewarm tea. The guard who brought this to him was the same female who had come into the wash room. She seemed indifferent to him now. He thanked her, but there was no reply.

'Eat and drink,' said another of his guards. 'You've got three minutes!'

Still chewing at the remains of the roll, Albanus was then bundled to the lift, the two guards propelling him by the arms. He was to face the inquiry panel again.

The members sat there at the long desk as if they had never left from the day before. Without any preamble, the Chairman said: 'Albanus Detrichen, when did you join the militia fighting against the forces of the State?'

Albanus had not expected this question and did not know at first how to reply. Whatever he said would condemn him. They clearly knew now of the years of his fighting against the Party. He could not have expected anything else. So, after being prompted a second time for an answer, he said simply: 'As soon as I could', which gained a gasp from the female member.

The Chairman remained passive. He simply looked at Albanus for a long five seconds and then said: 'You signed up with the Lietherhesk militia when you were eighteen, moved to the Wandergleski two years later, were promoted to sergeant when you joined the Zienderhorn, and served with them for the rest of the war, joining and re-joining a number of terrorist sections even after the State army had occupied the whole of our Eastern provinces.'

'I would not call them terrorist sections,' Albanus said dryly, 'but resistance groups'.

'Ah, yes. You were always the great hero. You fought and killed our men. You loved the war. You only stopped your killing when you realised the only future for you, if you were not to starve, lay in the City, and so you inveigled yourself into the Party to make a new career for yourself.'

The Chairman's calmness had ended. His voice took on a higher note as he slammed his fist down upon the desk. 'And so you prospered for a while until our agents caught up with you. You even used those poor, damned Christians – a hopeless idealistic sect, if there ever was one, who worship non-violence while practising bodily perversions and corruptions – as a cover for yourself. You are a fraud and a phoney, and a dangerous man, Albanus Detrichen. And so we have caught you at last. The question is what shall we do with you?'

Albanus said nothing. His heart was beating faster, his mind full of thought. Somewhere deep within him a dark shaft was jabbing at him – Is that true? Is that really what I did? And then, as rapidly as the thought arose, the answer – so clear and certain – filled his soul. Of course not.

Everything they say is lies. I have learnt of the mercy of Jesus Christ. He is the only one – mortal or divine – I will allow to judge me. I came to Christ seeking salvation, having learnt of him from the priest, have been baptised into his faith, and now wish to carry forward his sacred truth so all too can know him and understand his peace. I – Albanus – am a servant of Christ now, and my past – good or bad, as it may have been – is of no further consequence. These people before me, however, think otherwise. I cannot blame them. They have their own part to play. For all is ordained. I understand that now, as the priest has told me.

'I *do* believe'.

The last words he said out loud, causing the woman on the panel to call out. 'What do you believe?' And another too: 'You maggot. When you were a fighter, I might have had some understanding of you. But now, when you seek to subvert us through tales too stupid even for a child to believe in, I have none.'

'You think *that*,' said Albanus, stung out of his calm at last. 'You should open your mind a little and reflect on what is the meaning of your life, what purpose do *you* serve?'

'We are servants of the State,' another panel member responded. 'That is our purpose. Our leader is the President, who holds more power than your wonderful Christ, or whatever he is called – your tinpot, crazy god – will ever have. Our duty is to root out the insidious evil that assails the State from people like you who seek to do it harm.'

'We shall see then who has the greater power,' said Albanus, his calmness restored.

'Yes, we shall, indeed,' said the Chairman. 'Most definitely so. And I know who that will be. Albanus Detrichen, you will now be sent to trial.' He added, in a voice lowered to a venomous hiss. 'And, I have to tell you, unless your attitude changes drastically, I don't give much for your chances.'

'My life is not in your hands but in God's,' Albanus said, turning his back.

He was returned to his cell. He was now given a thin rubber mat to lie upon, which little improved his comfort. And he was allowed a collapsible chair with a seat made of webbing to sit upon during the long hours of the day. Every third day he was taken to the wash room. His food was very intermittent and he learnt to ignore the hunger and the thirst. From the chair, he was able to tear off two strips of the webbing, which he tied together to make a cross. Many of the long hours he had to endure, he spent in contemplation, looking upon the cross, wondering where the priest was, and Icheka and Janita, and others of the congregation, hoping they were all safe. And he thought too of his father, in wonder that he was still alive, and longing to look upon his face again – if only for the last time.

18

One day – it must have been some ten days after he was first imprisoned and cross-examined – his cell was entered suddenly by a uniformed man he had not seen before, in company with one of the regular guards. He was lying on his rubber mat to sleep, as he had judged that it was now night time, although it was hard to tell night from day owing to the irregularity of the routines he was subject to. The guard roused him with a shout, and he began to struggle to his feet, aware of the visitor standing over him. When he was able to focus on him, he saw he wore the elaborate, decorated uniform of the Presidential Guard – a light blue uniform with much gold braid on the jacket lapels and epaulettes, and with a peaked, high-brimmed cap, adorned with the silver Presidental star.

'You are to come with me,' this man said, who from the authority with which he spoke and acted was surely of officer rank.

'Where do we go?'

'It is not for you to ask.'

'Will I be returning here?'

'A prisoner does not ask questions. You obey.'

'Of course.'

Despite all his resolutions and long contemplations, Albanus felt a flutter of fear. Was he to be taken somewhere to be disposed of in secret. No one would ever know what had happened to him. This was not the ending he had imagined, the one he had understood God wished for him. Still, God was with him and would guide him, whatever was to happen.

Another guard came into the cell and flung a cloak at him. 'You will need this. It is cold outside.'

So he was to leave this prison within the police headquarters. But to go where? He bent to put on his shoes, also returned to him, then pulled on the cloak over his tunic. It was a thick, black cloak of high quality with a waterproofed outer surface. It tied at his throat and chest, and fell to his knees. Perhaps it had belonged to an earlier prisoner. Had the priest's cape been kept similarly, perhaps to be used as evidence against him?

He was marched at speed along the corridors, guards surrounding him, the Presidential guardsman striding out in front. They came to an outer court, which was lit by floodlights, the first time Albanus had been in the open air since he had arrived here. Rain, swept by a strong wind, beat against his face and body, before he was pushed onto the back seat of a large, black car. Other Presidential guardsmen climbed in on either side of him. In front, separated by a glass screen, were the driver and the officer who had come to the cell. The car smelt of scent. He wondered who had last been carried in it.

The windows were blacked out. Albanus could see nothing as they drove away. The drive was smooth, the car engine scarcely discernible; they seemed to glide along, as if sliding on ice, even the potholes and sunken gratings in the roads made no more than a small vibration. This must be an imported car, Albanus thought. The State does not make vehicles of this quality. Perhaps the State President uses it himself. And then a sudden realisation. Was he, in fact, being taken before the President himself?

They had stopped. Had they arrived? The guardsmen remained motionless beside him. In front, heads were tilted forward, clearly watching something that Albanus could not see. He sensed a further short movement of the car forward, then it stopped again. The doors were abruptly pulled open from outside.

'Out! Out! was shouted at him, as the guardsmen around him leapt out too. He stood under a glass canopy flooded by bright electric light. He could see the furious rain striking the canopy in showers of silver darts swept out of the blackness beyond. A blast of wind tore suddenly at his cloak, and he had to press his arms hard down to hold it in place. Then he was being led inside.

Down long corridors with plain white walls, punctuated by black doors from which the occasional face stared out, he passed with his escort of guards. They wore steel-capped boots which clashed on the stone floors. Then the stone turned to carpet and they arrived in a broad hall, lined with oak panelling and hung with many pictures, some he saw of ships, and others of red-coated soldiers fighting. A mounted cavalryman reared out of one picture as if he were about to charge into the room itself.

A man was awaiting them there, dressed in the formal style of an earlier age. He wore a jacket with long green tails, a white waistcoat, and white pantaloons, which ended in silken stockings, ringed by black, ribboned garters. When Albanus was pushed before him, he tut- tutted loudly. '

Take off the cloak,' he commanded. '. You can't wear that in here, not to....' He didn't complete the sentence.

Albanus obeyed, thinking I can do nothing else but obey these people. But I was right. This *is* the Presidential Palace, and it looks as if I am about to be brought before the President himself. But for what reason?

Some page or other, if such was his title, had been sent away at a run and returned with a dark-coloured jacket, embroidered on the cuffs and lapels with a golden pattern of swirls and curls. It was given to Albanus, who pulled it on. It was a little large across the shoulders for him.

'Much better. Much more suitable,' muttered the man with the green tails.

Albanus was now led forward by him through further rooms of ever-increasing grandeur, coming to one that was set with a long dining table, laden with fine china, heavy silver cutlery, and crystal jugs and goblets, with two enormous glass chandeliers overhead hanging low, suspended from a painted ceiling by wires like ships' cables.

At the far end of this room was a small, plain door, set between enormous framed portraits, one of a man in military uniform with curling moustaches and the other of a lady in a shining green dress, holding a rose in one hand. Albanus noticed the last picture, in particular, as it was the first indication of femininity he had seen in this place.

The green jacketed man, who – Albanus realised now – must be the steward to the palace, or the chamberlain, or have some other fancy title, knocked on the plain door, bending forward, his ear against the wood. Eventually, satisfied, he pushed it open, disappearing inside. He re-appeared almost at once, signalling the guardsmen who stood by Albanus to bring him forward. Albanus was then urged through the door, the guardsmen standing back. Presumably, Albanus thought, there will be others inside to seize hold of me, should I suddenly.....suddenly, do what? Run at......run at whom? Am I about to come face to face with the President?

The light was low. It was a small room lined with dark panelling. There were no guards. At the far end was a desk. Behind the desk, rising to his feet, was indeed the State

President. He was wearing a light-grey uniform jacket, which looked eerily luminous in the half-light: it was emblazoned with medal ribbons. In his right hand was a pistol, levelled at Albanus's chest.

He was a thick-set man of middle years with a heavy moustache – without doubt the man in the portraits outside, and the lady there, his wife. With thinning hair and reddened cheeks, this was the well-weathered face of someone long inured to the outdoors, who very likely enjoyed his drink.

Seeing the pistol pointed at him as steady as a rock, Albanus stood stock still. There was no where he could escape to, even if he had so wished. Well, get it over with then. I am ready to die, although I did not believe it would be like this – were his racing thoughts.

The President spoke. It was a deep rumble of a voice, a little slurred. Had he already been at his drink then? At the club, Albanus had picked up one or two scurrilous rumours about the President's drinking, delivered from behind cupped hands, only after the rumour-spreader himself had imbibed more than he should. No sober man spread stories about the President, particularly those not to his credit.

'Why do you hate me so much, Mr......' – he checked a note on his desk – '.....Mr. Detrichen?'

Albanus said nothing. He could see the President's finger curled over the trigger. He could rush him, flattening himself on the desk, grabbing upwards for the pistol. But this was a man used to firing. He would not miss. And anyhow, hearing the commotion, the guards would be in as quickly as any shot, and he dead in an instant.

'Did you hear me? Why do you hate me? You have been a soldier. A very good soldier, I have learnt. I could use men like you. You have joined the Party, I understand. So, why be so against me when the State could benefit from your skills?'

'I do not hate you, sir. Christianity teaches us to love, not hate. But your Party seeks to crush my faith and I oppose you for that reason.'

'Come now, all that is dreaming. I am a man of reality, as you must have been to have fought my armies so long and survived. A nation has to be tough to march forward. It needs discipline and obedience. That's what I look for in men, not the damaging dreams of fools, who only bring weakness.'

There was another long silence. Albanus did not know what to say. He did not wish to antagonise this man any further: he seemed impervious to any message of compassion.

The President slowly lowered the pistol, then pulled out a drawer of the desk and placed it inside, pushing the drawer back in again. He held up his hands. 'See, I am unarmed now. I am not afraid of you. I do not need angels to look after me.'

'No, sir. But you have guards outside. I have nothing. And, sir, although I may fear at times what is to come to me, in truth, I tell you, I am not afraid of you, or of any of your men.'

The President made a grunting noise in his throat, which some might have thought expressed irritation or disbelief, but which Albanus realised, much to his surprise, more likely expressed approval.

'Come, sit before me,' the President said, resuming his seat behind the desk. 'Pull up one of those chairs.'

Albanus selected a high-backed, ornate chair at the side of the room, and, pulled it forward, as he was asked. How extraordinary is this situation, he thought. This man can show harshness, but can be most civil too. Yet I know he will not weaken in his beliefs. And neither will I. If I did not know he dwelt in evil, seized the land of others, murdered and maimed to achieve his ends, I might well have worked with him once, for he has the strength and drive to achieve things, the sort of character I have always admired.

And I have done bad things too, so perhaps we are really two of a kind. Only, I have now learnt of the peace of Christ, which is by a million times a greater and a finer thing than all that this man and I, conjoined in a cause, would ever have done in the world, whether for good or evil. Christ's truth, I know now, must be the path for all of us – for mankind itself – into the future.

There came a sharp knocking at the door, and the head of the Guard commander looked in, searching the room with his eyes. 'Is all well, Sir?'

'Get out! Get out! You think I cannot look after myself!' The President's face was suffused with sudden fury. The head disappeared abruptly, like a rabbit into its hole. The rage as quickly left the President's face as it had come. 'My men fear for themselves as much as for me,' he said calmly. 'If you assassinated me, they would all be killed in turn for neglect of their duty. So you see, you must not do that.' He guffawed, spittle flecking his lips, which he wiped away with the back of his hand.

'That is not something I would do,' Albanus said. 'I am a man of peace now.'

'And you seek to make a personal sacrifice, I think. I believe those of the faith you profess call it a martyrdom.'

'If necessary, sir, I would go to my maker in such a way; and I tell you, sir, with peace in my heart.'

'Then I cannot allow it, Albanus Detrichen. You would be far more useful to me if you worked for me, for the State.'

'I have already done that, sir, abandoning the principles I fought for. I regret having done so now.'

'Why?'

'Because I have learnt of a far greater cause to live for.'

'And to die for?'

'If needs be, yes. I would die for the faith of our Lord Jesus

Christ. I tell you, sir, if you do not see the power of God when he is before you, you will not be able to see at all.'

There was a pause while the President looked at him steadily. His eyes were a flinty, light blue. They seemed to be boring deep into him, as if to seek out his faults, his weaknesses.

'You know...' the President spoke, breaking a silence that had seemed to last forever, so that, despite all his resolutions, Albanus had begun to feel uneasy, his determinations replaced by sudden doubts at the edge of his vision, flickering like fire. Do I really know what I am bringing myself to? Why I am doing so? But he had the answer at once, and felt sure again. By his own decision, he had helped the priest to escape, and had sacrificed himself, in order that God's messenger might yet spread his message to other people, so that they too could receive the joy and peace of Christ.

'...You should know,' the President began again, 'I am surprised that a man of your strengths and abilities has been so led astray by the one we really seek, in order, it appears, that *he* (not *you*) should escape arrest – at least for the present. I would allow *him* no mercy. For he is the true spreader of this mischief that has begun to infest certain of our people once again. The dullards who work for the State should have caught him long ago, not you. You are a fish I would easily throw back into the sea and allow to swim free again, if you would only express some regret for what you have done, and at the same time return your allegiance to the State. Of course, you know well, of whom I speak. You have been seen with him at your own house. He is...' he looked down again at the sheet of paper before him on the desk '....one known as Amphibalus, who calls himself a priest, and has long troubled us' He thrust his head forward over the desk. 'You are not a priest too, are you Albanus Detrichen?'

'No, sir. I am not.'

'But you have known this Amphibalus for some time?'

'Yes, sir. I have. He has instructed me in the faith of Christ.' Albanus knew he could admit this. It would make no difference now to the priest's safety.

'And where is he at present?'

'I do not know. If I did, sir, I would not tell you.'

The President resumed his silent study of Albanus's face. 'You do realise I could order you to be *made* to talk?' he said at last, his tone now much harder. 'There *are* ways.'

Albanus, realising that a change in their conversation had come, did not answer. He felt his own weaknesses burdening him again. He feared once more.

The President rose to his feet. Albanus stood as well. The two men stood facing each other, only a few feet apart.

'You are a brave man, Albanus. A soldier. We probably fought each other at some time on the same field. I respect that.'

'I thank you, sir. It is easy, I believe, to fight an enemy you can see, but not so easy to fight against one that comes in words and thoughts. Christianity, I wish to fight for now, and I shall keep my fight going for as long as I can – but with words, not weapons.'

'And so I must stop you, Albanus. It is so set. It is done. There is nothing else I can do for you then. I have tried to give you another way, which is why I have taken the trouble to see you and speak with you face-to-face, not a privilege, you understand, I allow to many. Now I must let my Guard know I am still alive and have not lost my reason.'

He raised his voice and called out, 'Come!'

Immediately, the door was opened and two guardsmen rushed in to seize Albanus by the arms and begin to pull him back towards the door. The President raised his hand to make them stop.

'When you leave here, Albanus, I will be unable to protect you further. This was your chance, your only chance. You will go before our Chief Judge next, and what he will say and do is inevitable. I wash my hands of you now, do you understand?'

'Yes, sir, I do.'

As he was led from the room, he heard the President muttering out loud, 'Such a fool. Such a bloody waste of a man. I could have made use of him. And so we all fall...we all must fall in time.'

Returned to his cell, the next day Albanus was surprised to receive a much thicker, pneumatic mattress, with a pillow too, to lay on his floor, and a more comfortable chair, well-cushioned. He did not know the reason for these better conditions. Had the President, himself, intervened? But why should he? Albanus had turned down his offer of life over death? Perhaps in that lay the reason. Was better treatment given to those already condemned to die?

The food he received now was also of better quality, and was served to him on a tray in his cell at regular hours. He was also allowed to use a flushable toilet next to his wash room, so all in all he felt quite the hotel guest. He even had some books to read, delivered to him, without his asking, by the female guard who had seen him naked and vulnerable when he first arrived. He thought her gaze upon him was lit by something of humanity now. He was not sure, though, because she said very little. But it raised his spirits to think so. Guards did not generally speak with prisoners. They gave them orders, and led them hither and thither – that was all.

Occasionally, he was taken outside into a courtyard ringed by high walls and open to the sky. It was not a space used by other prisoners, but one, it seemed, mainly for the recreation of the guards. There was an area of grass here, surrounded by orange flowers, and even a concrete pool at the centre, in which some golden fish glided amongst tufts of emerald green weed. He was allowed to sit on a seat nearby and gaze into the water.

Jesus had said, 'I will make you now fishers of men.' Albanus had no doubts of the course he had to follow. He retained the cross he had made of the webbing slips and kept it by his side. His fear had retreated to a small, nagging presence at the back of his mind.

19

It was only a short time that Albanus would spend in these more comfortable conditions. On the afternoon of the fifth day after his meeting with the President, he was told, through a brief typed note brought to him by a guard, that his trial would take place the next day at the City Law Courts. This complex had been completed only recently to a brutalist design by a foreign architect, with its various towers and glass-fronted blocks like a child's bricks dumped down, then randomly piled up again. The concrete facing panels were ribbed and fissured like the flat-topped, geological rocks once trodden by the dinosaurs.

The very short notice of the trial gave little time for Albanus to prepare himself. No attorney appeared to represent him, and, when he asked for one through a guard, there was no response at all. He doubted if the request had been passed on. The charge against him was treason. That word was baldly stated on the notification given him. Perhaps defendants accused of treason were not allowed legal help. He would have to defend himself.

In fact, he preferred to represent himself, rather than have someone else speaking for him, twisting his words around, turning them inside out, watering them down to make them into something he had not meant. He would face his accusers straight on. He would answer them directly, without fear of speaking the plain truth, although by that he would assuredly be found guilty – and the sentence for treason was death. He did not expect any mercy. Now he had rebuffed the President's approach to him, he did not think there was any mercy left to be offered. He would never compromise his Christian beliefs.

Would those words he had spoken so passionately to the President be repeated in the court to be used against him? He hoped so. They were his beliefs. He could not make them any clearer, however he spoke them. They would surely gain him the death he now sought, for it was written so, and this present was just a brief period he must pass through before going on to find the risen Christ in glory.

That evening, the female guard told him he must be ready to leave the next day by eight of the clock. 'You will be woken well before that time. You should wear the jacket you now have over your tunic: it will be better you wear that than the prison clothes we would give you otherwise. I will let you have some socks, though, for the weather is chilly at present.'

Albanus was touched. Fussing in this way over him was likely beyond her strict duties. 'What is your name?' he asked.

'We are not permitted....'

She made to leave him, then came back. 'Sherdra,' she said. ''My name is Sherdra.' And, then quickly and low, so he could scarcely hear: 'Pray for me.'

'I will, my sister. God looks upon you and knows you.'

She said no more. After she had brought him the socks, she disappeared. He did not see her again. But he knew she would be safe, and he kept his prayer for her in his head, repeating it from time to time, 'My God, look to your servant Sherdra, to keep her safe. She has helped me at danger to herself, bringing me comfort, and she is truly of the blessed ones.'

The next morning he was roused very early by a guard banging at the door. After being taken for a shower, he dressed himself, managing to tie his makeshift cross at his chest beneath his tunic, where he could feel it against his flesh but it would not be seen. He drew on the fawn-coloured socks, which were long and reached up below his tunic to above his knees, and then pulled on the embroidered jacket he had been given at the Presidential Palace; it was lined with red silk and he wondered whose it had been. Someone high up in the Party, he assumed, perhaps someone who had fallen from favour since.

Now he was dressed for the day, however strange his appearance might appear in the court. It would be understood, he was sure. Who would attend the court? Were ordinary citizens allowed to be there to watch the proceedings? Or was it held behind closed doors? There were so many things he did not know. This day would soon provide him with the answers.

He was taken to the City Law Courts not in a closed van but a type of people carrier with darkened windows that had cushioned bench seats. Two guards sat either side of him. He could see out, if obscurely, but no one outside could see in. As they passed through the busy streets with sirens wailing, other vehicles froze in front of them, then edged towards the kerb to get out of the way. Oncoming traffic was held up by policewomen, their white-sleeved arms flourishing like wind sails. On both sides of the street, pedestrians stopped to stare at the vehicle going past, motorcycle outriders accompanying it. Albanus thought, what a performance just for me. If they'd asked me, I could have walked quietly there by myself. I would have enjoyed the fresh air and the exercise.

When they reached the Law Courts, they drove to the rear of the building and entered a bleak-looking courtyard, on one side of which some piled metal crates spilled out rubbish. Scavenging birds hovered and fought above them, the sound of their squawking unheard within the vehicle. Rounding these crates, they came to a large, open gateway in the wall of the main building, beyond which a concrete ramp descended steeply to the depths below. They followed this ramp down without pause, then at its base weaved their way between huge, square pillars brightly lit by spotlights. In an open area, they stopped.

Doors sprung open. A guard ordered Albanus out. His wrists were seized immediately and clamped behind his back. He was frogmarched through a door, along a narrow corridor, and into a cell – a very small cell, he saw, but with a recess along one side that formed a ledge where he could sit, or, if needs be, lie.

The door to the cell crashed shut and he was alone. He looked around. There was little to see. The walls were bare and seemed to be made of metal. They were painted grey. Why metal and not concrete? He thumped at one with his fist. There was no booming sound of any sort. It was as rigid as rock. The steel sheets must be many inches thick.

He sat on the ledge, his head bent forward, as the recess in the wall was only a few feet high. He felt numb, his mind for once devoid of thought. Yet he should prepare himself now for what he would say at his trial, and in what manner he would do so.

Should he be humble? Or should he be truculent; unbowed; undaunted, regretting nothing? And then he decided, I shall be none of those things. I shall be myself with the word of God on my tongue. And Christ himself, the Son of God, will be beside me to help me speak his truth. I know that because I have been told so, and I *believe*.

He did not have long to wait. There came a great clatter of keys and bolts, sounding to him like a rattling from hell. Get a grip, he told himself. Remember the faith. Show no fear. The cell door crashed open.

There were four guards this time in a different uniform, of the boiler-suit type and a deep maroon in colour. Two appeared to be women, but it was hard to tell, because of the loose nature of their uniforms and their faces were round and flat and unpainted. They all wore black, peaked caps. These must be the particular guards of the Law Courts, he assumed.

'Up and out! Move! Move!' a guard yelled in his face. The voice was shrill. He looked into the hard face. Yes, a woman for sure.

'Where are we going?'

She slashed at his arm with the small cane she carried. 'To the court. Where do you think? For your trial, dimwit!' Her face was thrust forward against his. Spots of her saliva spattered his face. The other guards tittered.

'Well, take me there then,' he said, as calmly as he could.

Once through the cell door, the guards formed a tight group about him, and they marched him in a jerky, goose-stepping rhythm down the corridor, up some stairs, and into an empty, high-ceilinged room, the walls of which were bare, other than for a number of large posters proclaiming patriotic messages. 'Love your Party. Love your State', Albanus read, as he was halted beneath one. The picture above the legend was of a teary-eyed maiden in Party clothing looking out across yellow corn fields.

The guard who had struck at him was peering through a gap in double-leafed doors at the far end of the room. 'Come!' she called, and Albanus was marched through the doors and into a broad, open space beyond.

Blinking his eyes in the sudden glare of electric lighting, he realised he was standing in a court room. A curved row of seats faced him, each seat with a table in front of it, and above, two further tiers of seating, divided by a central stairway. Many faces stared down at him. Dominating the centre of the highest tier, above the stairway, was an ornate, single chair, with a canopy above and square pillars each side, upon which the various emblems of the State were displayed. The chair was empty.

Albanus was led to a low wooden-walled structure that looked like an open-topped box. Inside was a backless bench on which he was told to sit. His guard unfastened his hands, and retired to stand behind him. Albanus was intrigued now, wondering rather than fearful. A process such as this he had never encountered before. The watching faces must all be of Party officials. It seemed there was no jury of his fellow citizens present.

'All stand!' a voice roared out, and, to a great shuffling of feet, everyone rose as the judge entered the court room from a side door. Climbing the stairway, his trailing red robe followed by several officials in formal black suits, he took up his position in the canopied, central chair, high and dominant in the room. He was wearing an old-fashioned wig, long and curled to his shoulders, such as Albanus had only ever seen in films before.

The Party has created its new State, he thought, but they appear to live still by some of its old traditions. Let me hope they live by justice as well – yet he knew that to be impossible now. The President had already told him so. His life was already draining from him fast, like a man who has cut his own wrists and awaits finality.

'All seated!'

Albanus, having just risen with the rest, collapsed downwards again, as did all now, the judge too, filling his great chair with his red-robed body.

Albanus was called back to his feet at once. The judge rasped out from his throne: 'Prisoner at the bar! You must stand. Do not seat yourself again until directly told to do so.'

'Yes, sir.'

He would obey their petty demands, follow their corrupt rituals. He did not recognise this court. It had no power over him. But he would not tell them that, not yet, anyhow. He would play out this game as they wanted it played, and with dignity too.

'You should address me as "my lord."'

'My apologies, my lord.'

'Albanus Detrichen, you have been brought here to answer a grave charge – indeed the gravest charge of all – which is that of treason to the State. How do you plead?'

'Not guilty, my lord.' There was a rustle about the court.

'Who represents you here?'

'I have no one, my lord. I represent myself, with God beside me.'

There were sighs and murmurs at the last words, even some stifled gasps.

The judge leant forward, a finger raised: 'Is that wise, Mr. Detrichen? And I must tell you before we go any further, I will not have you bringing your blasphemous religion into my court. We will, of necessity, have to refer to it, since it forms the basis of the charge against you, but I will allow no expression beyond that. Do you understand?"

'I do, my lord. I shall obey, of course, but you – this court – will know nonetheless what is in my mind. You can silence me outwardly but not inwardly. I have been offered no counsel, my lord. I have been held in prison, have been told of no rights I might have, and have been given no information at all, let alone help, concerning this trial, of which I am wholly ignorant.'

There came a further murmuring in the court.

'I have the power to silence you in every way,' the judge declared grimly, stabbing his finger.. 'Regarding your lack of counsel, that I fear is your affair and not now the concern of this court. You should have challenged the matter earlier.'

'I did not know anything of it, my lord. I was not even told I would be brought to trial until yesterday. Nonetheless, I am ready now to make my own defence.'

The judge was speaking to another red-gowned figure at his side – a woman, Albanus deduced, from the length of her hair seen about the absurd pie-crust of a hat she wore. After what seemed a lengthy period, the judge turned back to Albanus. 'Your complaint is recognised. It will be investigated later.'

That is ridiculous, he thought. This whole procedure is preposterous, just a pretence at legality, a superficial veneer that covers an utter corruption of power. By the time my complaint is 'investigated, I shall likely have been put to death – far from this perversion of existence that I have fought so long against, only to have embraced it myself, briefly, vainly and foolishly. I die to atone for my own falsehoods and wrongs as much as for my Christian faith. Oh Lord, he prayed inwardly, help me through this trial, the real trial beyond this court, the far greater trial that is to come.

The sequence of events that passed now were to Albanus like scenes from a film, in which he had a role to act out, but which, as a player, held little reality for him. It was a story he hoped would be brought to an end as soon as possible.

A prosecutor, a black-cloaked woman with a scrawny wig flattened on her head like a cow pat – Albanus thought she might be the same woman as had been so hostile to him at the first hearing – outlined the case against him. Witnesses were brought who testified against him. One was his next door neighbour, who spoke of gatherings in his house and lewd goings-on there that she had observed by peeping through a window – touchings and fondlings, and kneelings by the defendant before another man that suggested *fellatio*, men kissing men, and worse, practices that indicated sodomy was to be committed – a criminal offence by itself. It was well known that all suchlike behaviour was a Christian abomination, and she gave witness to it reluctantly, not to harm her neighbour as such, but for the good of the Party and the State, that they should be eradicated.

She also reported that the man she had seen with the defendant was dressed as a priest (she understood that now, he 'one of those Christian demons who spread their vileness amongst us', although she had been unsure at the time), and that she had seen the same man leaving the house, whom it was clear now had been Albanus Detrichen, dressed to appear as the priest.

She has made up most of that, Albanus thought – likely paid to do so – for the priest was never at my house, nor any other man, until that last day. What she says, however, of seeing me leaving the house dressed as the priest is likely true. I suspected she was watching.

It grew worse, full of more lies. Members of his own work team were produced, who told of notes they had found which spoke of his Christian assignations, and phone calls overheard. One young woman, who had been amongst those he had taken to the football match at the Arena, declared on oath that he had taken her into a toilet cubicle and put his hands on her breasts and up her skirt, and after the match he had forced her to lie with him in the public park and have sex with her, although she was yet a virgin and engaged to a State soldier.

'How could I deny my Party supervisor?' she had wailed to the court, and there had been a hubbub of commiseration, with ferocious looks directed at Albanus. He stood in his wooden box – he had not been allowed to sit even during the witness statements – watching her in amazement. How had she been bribed to tell such lies? She had been one he had liked best, and he had recommended her for promotion. Why such betrayal?

Another office worker, a cleaner with whom he had often swapped jokes when he stayed late after the official day's work ended, with much hesitation and embarrassment at first, told the court she knew he masturbated in the office after hours, for she had found certain stains on the carpet beneath his desk that had likely come from such a practice. Despite his resolution, Albanus broke into laughter at this, and, when allowed for once to cross-question, asked: 'How then did you learn to recognise such stains? Where and when did you see the like before?' The cleaner had retired confused, while the court hissed its shame at Albanus's levity.

More serious were the witnesses who had seen him with the priest at his baptism, although it was not referred to as such in the court; rather as a 'naked frolic in the river', or other words to that effect. One witness had seen him walking in the City streets with the priest. His final act of disguising himself as the priest was put to him as his greatest crime of all, by its deliberate attempt to deceive the security forces of the State while carrying out their duties – an act indeed of treason. He was told by the prosecutor that as a Party member himself such a contrived duplicity made the offence even worse; it alone was enough to have him convicted as a traitor.

Albanus was relieved, however, that no witness appeared to give evidence about the comings and goings at Nanta's flat, which he had thought very likely. He had been most worried that other arrests might have been made – Nanta and Janita and Icheka, for instance, the last particularly vulnerable because of her own position with the Party. The comings and goings at Nanta's block of flats must have been obvious to other residents He could only think these people were so frightened of the State, and perhaps had other activities to hide, that they were willing to turn a blind eye to anything suspicious, unless it concerned them personally.

He was as equally relieved that there was no reference to Icheka at his house: he would have expected the snooping neighbour to have reported on her too. The neighbour could only have assumed her presence was perfectly normal, although likely a cause of irritation and some jealousy to her. Perhaps the inventions she had already spoken – contrived very likely with the Party prosecutor – had been sufficient for this trial. Or possibly she might be saving up further information for future use if, for example, there was a second hearing – for more payment, very likely. Anything was possible in this corrupt State.

As there had been no mention in the court of other arrests of Christians being made in the City, or beyond, he kept the hope that both Icheka and Janita were still free and safe, and the priest himself. Where would he be now? Hopefully, far from the City, and now well-disguised, because the search for him would surely be relentless.

Albanus's long service with militia units against the forces of the State was put to the court by the prosecutor in some detail. The President's amnesty had not covered those who had joined what the State termed 'irregular terrorist groups', which Albanus was now accused of having belonged to. The prosecutor was able to tell of Albanus's long-held hostility to the State, which recent events had shown to be still as strong as ever. It was clear, she said, that he had only latterly become an employee of the State in order to mask his continuing campaign against it. Even the pretence of his Christianity – as she termed it – was a device to undermine the State further. She told the court she didn't think Mr. Detrichen had an ounce of 'any religion that spoke of peace and golden clouds with singing angels' in his whole body.

There were titters in the court room at that, while Albanus swayed unsteadily in his box, his legs aching, trying to keep his rising temper at bay. He traced with his fingertips the makeshift cross against his chest, and he thought of Janita and the quiet love she had shown him, and how she bore herself so strongly and bravely despite the handicap of her crippled leg, and he felt his strength returning.

After nearly three hours, it was all over. Albanus was allowed to be seated, as the judge called for the judgement of the court to be considered and a verdict reached. This process was carried out within the court room. The many heads along the rows of seats, Albanus realised now, were in fact those who would decide his fate. They were marking paper slips that were then gathered up and taken to the judge in his lofty perch. There was much to'ing and fro'ing, and whispering along the wooden-fronted rows, and then the task was done. The judge pulled on a black cap over his wig, while an official intoned 'All stand.'

Albanus scrambled once more to his feet, his heart beginning to race, although he realised what was to come and had prepared himself for it. It was obvious from the black cap the judge now wore, but would have been clear to him, anyhow. They wanted to be rid of him. This court room, and the absurd fantasy of justice just played out here, was now hardening to the grim, hard reality of his sentence – to be one of death, assuredly. It was the natural end of all this madness, all this posturing, all this pretence.

In his mind, he was back on the battlefield, where reality came not in words but in sprays of razor-sharp steel, in showers of mushrooming earth, in wet ditches, blood and shredded flesh, the huge, dark stains of explosions puncturing the yellow fields. He could face a reality like that. He had done so during seven long years of war. He could face this present reality too.

The last chapter of his life would end as it had begun when he joined up to fight – in the fear of death and in death itself. Only there was no fear now, for he *believed*. He would die in the knowledge of the Lord Jesus Christ, with whom he would soon come face to face, and by whom he would be judged – not by this court of evil charlatans whose only aim was to live out a lie, to whom evil and brutality were strengths, and love and mercy merely weakness.

The chief judge remained seated to deliver his verdict, everyone else in the court room was standing.

'Albanus Detrichen, this court has unanimously found you guilty, on three separate charges of high treason – treason against the State, treason against the laws and natural customs of our people, treason against the person of the State President himself.'

'How the last?' thought Albanus. How the last? Yet what difference does it make. They will all rot in hell.

'Your sentence is death by firing squad, at a time and place to be decided. That is all.'

The court before him suddenly seemed to dissolve, and he was looking again into that misty void he remembered from those previous times when this had happened, the mist falling away to show another scene entirely – now he could see men in long, white robes, draped and folded about their bodies who stood before a man in armour with a dark wreath about his head, being seated in a great stone chair set on a raised platform. The shadows of columns swept across the view, as if a strong wind was blowing. Then the scene as quickly broke up, as the others had done, and he was back in the court again where he had just been sentenced to death. He was troubled more by what these recurring visions might mean than by the judge's voice still spelling out the last of his instructions for the winding-up of the court.

Albanus was seized by the guards behind him, his arms twisted back and cuffed. The many faces about the court room stared at him, some snarling, some sneering, most indifferent. As the guards hauled him away, his body felt uncertain of movement, drained of all energy. He stumbled while coming down from the box and hoped this did not show as weakness. He felt detached from the immediacy of what was happening: he did not know why. It was not the verdict and the sentence that had caused this. He had expected nothing less. It was something else, something much more complex than he could understand.

He was being led away to the death he had expected. Of another parallel death, distant in time, he knew nothing at all.

20

Albanus had been returned to his steel-walled cell at the Law Courts. His treatment was now far worse. Condemned prisoners of the State were regarded as if already dead. At least that was Albanus's conclusion, as one day followed another in his steel cell. He had always expected to meet harshness in prison, even physical brutality and beating, and had been surprised when earlier he had received concessions that spoke a little of humanity.

Nothing like that, however, penetrated these steel walls. No intervention by the President could possibly come now. He knew he was of little significance in the affairs of the State, just a passing irritation, perhaps. He would soon be forgotten entirely. But he put all such thinking aside. His course had been set. There was no uncertainty remaining. He knew what was to happen to him, if not yet when. It would not be long, however. Of that he was sure.

He slept flat on his back on the cell's narrow metal ledge, frightened of turning over in case he fell to the floor. They supplied him with a cork mat that was meant to soften the steel bed, but if anything it made it more uncomfortable than before. He had to bang at the cell door if he wanted the toilet, and often they would not come for an hour, or so. Meals were sparse and pushed at him through a hatch in the door. If he did not react in time to get hold of the dish, it would fall to the ground, and he would have to scrape up the contents with his fingers. Spilt liquid, he must lap up like a dog.

With plenty of time to ponder, Albanus was able to see clearly the other issues that were bound up in the death that was so soon to come to him. These were far greater than the death of one man alone, however noble and selfless it might be for the Christian cause. The love of Christ, the slow but steady growth of a religion of truth, was not a matter that could be so easily swept away by the State, its adherents punctured with bullets, their bodies burnt. The State might be able to do this for a while, but if Christians stood true to what they believed, then change *must* inevitably come, as had happened in Rome all those centuries before. Example was what was required, and a persistence of belief that never wavered, fearlessness too in confronting evil, and, at the extreme, personal sacrifice in a cause that was God's cause, and that of all humanity too. He felt sure his own sacrifice, and probably those of others to come, would in time succeed in overthrowing this rule of Satan, with God's church then re-established in its place.

How much better the State would be, Albanus thought, if it ruled with the morality of Christianity as its foundation. Information was hard to come by, but he had learnt from incautious comments by Party members he had overheard in the drinking halls and clubs that the outer world was still reluctant to accept this new, autocratic State that had emerged after a long, brutal war, one where any true democracy was still denied.

Of course, the Party published statistics – Albanus had been involved in producing many of these – that showed over 90% of the population supported the Party's rule. But statistics, as he well knew, could equally be contrived to show the exact opposite. If the Party were only able to demonstrate that its people were at least allowed to worship as they wished, according to their own consciences, then that surely would be a great step towards the State's eventual acceptance by the world's major powers, an acceptance that would certainly bring greater overseas investment and development for the benefit of all its people.

On the sixth day after his sentencing – as well as he could judge the passing of time – three male guards took him to a place where there was a thin dribble of water falling from a pipe, under which he was told to wash. As he stripped off his tunic, his make-shift cross was noted and ripped from his neck. One guard he had not seen before, fat and ugly, struck him in the face with his baton. 'You won't need that, you god loving c---!' He then railed at the other guards. 'Why hasn't he been searched?! Get out both of you! You're useless!'

Albanus washed away the blood oozing from his nose. Bloodied water flowed onto his chest, into his groin and down his legs. The fat guard pushed some clothing at him, brought by a uniformed woman. 'Take a look at him,' said the fat guard. 'This is Mr. f---ing Christ, who's going to save us with his blood.'

He's learnt something of Jesu then, Albanus thought, or he would not know those words. How did Satan get into him, so to corrupt him?

The woman was staring at Albanus. Her face was devoid of expression. What did she see? His suffering, his many battle scars, his drooping, bloodied penis?

'You fancy him, don't you, Zana?' laughed the guard. 'How about a night with him then? You hear that, prisoner. Would you like a last night of passion with Zana here before you're shot tomorrow?'

So that is it, thought Albanus. Tomorrow is to be the day. That's what they're cleaning me up for.

The woman had gone. The clothing brought to Albanus now was a coarse, flaxen-coloured tunic that almost reached the ground. It had been crudely repaired in three places across the chest, where huge white stitches pulled rents together. These areas were stained a darker colour, like rust.

The guard was still chuckling at his joke. 'Put it on. It's what you'll wear tomorrow. It's what the last poor sod wore when he was shot. He wasn't a religious nut like you, though. He was a porter at the hospital. Stole drugs and sold them on the street. They say he f----ed the matron to get them, but I can't believe that. She had an arse bigger than a pig's.'

He gave out a squeal of giggles. He is like a pig himself, thought Albanus, although that's very unfair to the animal.

He felt sick – sick at this evil that so easily danced about his ears, driving out the beauty of the world, the beauty of nature, the beauty of Christ – Christ, who was the Son of God, the creator of all things, even this vile sin-ridden guard whom once he – Albanus – would have crushed with a single blow. So he bore up against the guard, knowing he was of little account compared with what he must face tomorrow.

Back in his cell, an hour or so later there came another sudden clashing of keys and another entry, this time of a soldier in uniform, clearly an officer, from the gold stars on his epaulettes and the many coloured medal rows upon his chest. Beside him were two other men, in plain dark Party suits.

'Albanus Detrichen,' said the officer. 'This is to notify you that you will be taken from here at 08.00 hours tomorrow to the place of your execution. You are to be shot by firing squad in the Arena. The exact time is not yet set, but your execution will be after the army parades that are to be held in the morning. Tomorrow is the 22nd June, our State Day. The State President, himself, will be in attendance. Is all that clear to you?'

'It couldn't be clearer,' said Albanus, drily. A sense of unreality was settling over him again. He didn't feel frightened now, he was pleased to note, but he didn't like those feelings of unreality that had come to him occasionally He hoped he would not have any more of those strange visions. It seemed to be stress that brought them on, and surely there was little more stressful than the confirmation of one's own imminent death.

'Then I salute you,' said the officer. 'As a soldier who has fought bravely, although we were on opposite sides. Your other crimes do not mean you are not entitled to the respect of a fellow soldier.'

'I thank you for that consideration,' said Albanus, gravely. He felt a surge of emotion, knowing he must keep that under control as well. 'I would salute you too, sir, but I feel I am not adequately dressed.'

The officer clicked his heels and turned away. The two in grey suits now moved in. They wanted to know about the disposal of his effects.

'I have none,' he answered.

'And your body – your remains?' They were anxious, diffident even.

'Surely you will be disposing of those as you see fit. It will not matter to me, being dead.'

'But your relatives, sir? The President has said he is prepared to allow whatever reasonable is requested by your family, as long as there is no question of anything being set up at which other dissidents might gather. Normally, you see, sir, with executed traitors, the body is burnt and the ashes spread on the common tip.'

'I have no family'. And then he realised that was not true. Most joyously, his father was still alive. Where would he want his son's remains to be placed? His father's memory of him, and the love of his fellow Christians, was all he wished for. Where his dust was placed did not matter.

'Do as you like,' he said. 'The common tip seems fine.'

He felt sick now. He would like a drink of whisky or vodka, or anything with alcohol, the stronger the better. Even the weak beer of the State canteens would do.

The suited men left, and he had no further visitors. Some food was brought. It was better than usual – a type of hot stew that was surprisingly tasty. The drink was not whisky, though, only a rather murky looking water. He asked the guard, who checked on him later, what the time was, and she said it was close to midnight. He lay himself down on the narrow ledge bed. His face, bruised by the guard's baton, was sore, but the bleeding had stopped. He said the Lord's prayer over and over in his head. 'Our father, who art in Heaven, hallowed be thy name'.

'Oh, Lord, take this cup from me,' he prayed

After a while he slept.

21

They came for him at the time stated. He had been wakened at 07.00 by much clashing of feet beyond his cell door, sounds that penetrated even the thick steel. He was brought water to drink and bread – good bread, it was, with a thick crust that he washed down with the water. His mind was still. He said a prayer and was at peace with himself. He did not fear. He knew he would be going to his God today, and might pass through some pain – but it would be quick, and then he would be free.

He was allowed to shave, something that had been neglected these days since the trial. A guard stood with him at the small basin beyond his cell in case he should seek to cut himself in some impossible way with the thin, inset razor blade. There was a mirror above the basin, and he looked into his own face; his once tanned skin now had a pallor to it, although he hoped there was still colour enough in his face, so that he would not look scared. His high forehead and temples were framed by a tousled mop of fair hair, now darker than it once was. His last visit to a hairdresser had been some considerable time ago. His hair was thinner as well. Old age advancing. Well, old age was about to be stopped in its track. He felt a thud of his heart at that thought. His heart, too, its beat soon to be stilled.

Of course, he was scared! No mortal man could be anything else. Yet, with the blessed Christ beside him, he was determined not to show it. Even Christ on the cross, in all his suffering, had not been free of doubt in the extremity of his passion.

He had been given a loincloth to wear – perhaps so as not to offend any watchers if I fall, he thought wryly, not for my comfort, that is sure – and he pulled the patched tunic over it. He had nothing to wear on top of that now – his jacket had been taken – but he saw he had also been left a shawl, which he draped about the shoulders. At least he had his own shoes returned to him – those he had worn to his baptism – in which he could now tread out the last steps of his life.

I must look like a farm woman about to feed her hens, he thought. I would have liked to die in my soldier's uniform – now as a soldier of Christ, but it is not to be. It is after all not how a man looks that matters, but in what manner he dies. And I shall not disappoint those who watch, only those who might wish I cry out for mercy.

Soldiers were in his cell now, men in grey-green uniform, who would have the task of escorting him to the Arena. He was led out. He had not been handcuffed. As he passed down the long passage with its many steel doors, a thumping at the doors began, with the muffled sound of voices calling out. His fellow prisoners, whom he had scarcely ever seen, must know he was going to his death, and they were beating out a farewell – for him, or against him, he did not know. It did not matter. It was a companionship in death, and, despite himself, it brought a lump to his throat. He walked on stiffly upright, pretending indifference, with the guards' stamping step about him.

Outside the Law Courts, in the courtyard where he had been brought in, he had expected to be placed in a vehicle to be driven to his final destination at the Arena. However, it soon became clear he was to be marched there in a formal procession. The guard commander told him. 'Prisoner, prepare yourself. The people of the City have been told you will be paraded before them on this Day of the State. So the streets will be lined with many watching.'

'Do the people know of what I am condemned?' Albanus asked.

'Prisoner, they know of your treasons and your sentence.'

They have been told lies, Albanus thought. Am I to be shot in front of the people too?

The procession formed up in the courtyard. There was an armoured car at the front with an open truckload of soldiers behind, then came a file of soldiers bearing standards, with the flag of the State held high at their head, and, behind them, ranks of soldiers in combat clothing bearing assault rifles at the slope.

The guard party, of which Albanus was at the centre, followed these latter, and further behind, bringing up the rear, came two officers mounted on black horses. What a performance, just for me, Albanus thought. There are more troops here than our militia ever had in battle. So this then is what I fought so long for. Total obliteration! It was only a passing thought, a material rather than a spiritual realisation, but it shook him.

He prayed, his lips moving. 'Oh Jesu, who sees everything. Held me to bear up against this defeat of my body, only to think of you to the end, to the very end, in that final victory of my soul, when I shall be at your side. Amen. Amen.'

The procession was now moving out into the streets, Albanus's group following, the horses behind. Turning his head, he saw a horse rearing up, endangering its rider, who clung to its neck. That man has scarcely ridden before, he thought. Perhaps none of these soldiers has ever fought either.

The war is over. I am left. I have seen everything, but soon I will pass too. Perhaps some memory of me will remain.

The pavements were largely empty at first, but further into the centre of the City there were crowds, some men even holding up children to gain a better view. He began to pass between them, the soldiers beside him keeping step, he trying to match their pace, trying not to shuffle, keeping his body upright. It was hard, as he felt so strange, his head spinning. The people dissolved, then hardened again: there were colours, women with veils over their heads, hands raised, rattles in their hands, a sound of trumpets on the air, the crash of steel-shod booted feet, men in robes, bearded faces calling out; then they vanished and the real City street rushed back with the children riding piggy back.

Now shouts were coming to him. 'Goodbye, scumhead!' 'Your're getting what you deserve, traitor!' 'Where's your f---ing god now, arsehole?'

Yet others, he saw stood silently, even a few in tears. One called out fearlessly, 'God bless you, my son.' And he saw with amazement it was the priest, wearing a plain boiler suit; clean-shaven, but his dark face clear. So the priest was not far away in safety. He had returned already, as God must have told him to do. And near him, seen with an urgent sweep of Albanus's eye, was Icheka, her face lowered, weeping; and close to her Janita too, limping along behind the crowd, her hand waving at him. He heard her voice cry out, 'Remember, Albanus. Remember.'

He twisted his body backwards to keep her in sight for as long as possible. Who was that man she now stood beside? An elderly man, with a hand that was raised feebly to him, his face full of light. It was his father, for certain, come to watch his son go to his death. Albanus held his own hand up in recognition, so his father would know he had seen him.

His father's clear joy at seeing him, together with the love of the others, came to him as a physical force, flooding him with sudden, fierce delight, then great sadness. He bent his head so that the tears which suddenly flooded his eyes would not be seen. They must take much better care, he thought, or they will be recognised. It is remarkable that they still walk so fearlessly in the open. Yet he knew God would be looking after them. He had no doubt of that.

As the procession approached the Arena, the crowds lining the streets grew thicker. There were more angry cries here and much waving of fists. Police lined the pavements, making sure no one rushed at the traitor to deliver their own justice, although with the soldiers about Albanus, it would have been difficult to reach him. There are always crazed people seeking an instant of fame, he thought. What harm have I done any of them?

They came up to the walls of the Arena, and into the large, open forecourt with its patterned paving before the main entry doors. Here the crowds, for the present, had been kept away. They would be let in later to view the army parades and, after that, to witness the execution.

The execution was to be the highlight of the State Day. The crowds were exceptionally big because it was a holiday. Executions in public were rare, but, when they came, were very popular. Even children were allowed to attend. It was said it was good education for them, reinforcing what they were daily taught at school – that the State needed to be kept powerful and safe.

The procession halted at the edge of the forecourt, and broke up. The army vehicles were driven off, the marching soldiers dispersed, most of them climbing up into lorries that had been waiting to collect them. The horse riders and their mounts disappeared as well: Albanus did not see where.

Perhaps they were to be part of the coming show in the Arena – the show that was to include him as well!

He was prodded forward, and led into the building. His hands were now cuffed together, but this time at his front rather than behind. He was put into a room at the level of the Arena floor. He saw stencilled on the door, 'For maintenance staff only.'

The table in the room had been pushed against a wall and a stack of metal-framed chairs brought in. He sat on one with several guards watching him. He was brought a hot drink, which he was able to lift to his mouth with his fingertips, his hands tightly together as if he were praying. The drink tasted like coffee. He had not drunk coffee for years. It was only lukewarm, but very welcome. The sugar it contained helped revive him. Then he was given a sandwich of meat with tomato. He eat it hungrily. He had been half-starved of late. He needed food for strength when the time came.

The room had a window. He was allowed to look out of it, watched by his guards, who occasionally changed. One now was a woman. He could smell perfume on her. She looked a pleasing girl, with black hair tied up under her service cap. He smiled at her, but she looked away.

He thought of trees and meadows, and the long light on the grass looking towards the distant hills, as he had last seen the view from Janita's farm. And he thought of making love to a woman, and lying with her in the thick grasses, her hand in his, and staring up at the sky, wondering at the meaning of the world as it made its small track amongst the billion stars. He remembered all the many things he had loved, especially the comradeship of the war, when he felt he had come closest of all to the essence of existence – of survival and friendship and of risking and giving one's own life to save others.

Wasn't that what he was doing now? – offering up his life

so that others might live and have peace and joy about them, without the fear that came with steel-capped boots and guns. He thought of all these things, rather than thinking directly of God, but that did not seem to matter at this time, because, of course, God made all those things so dear to him that he had enjoyed. Whatever, and whenever, you loved, then you loved God too.

He thought of the priest and he thought of his murdered mother and brothers, and he remembered the small frail figure of his father, yet living by God's miracle, who had been so determined to look upon his son one last time. He thought of Janita, who might have become his one big love, and he thought of Inceka, who had given her body to him and been such a loyal and good friend. It was she who had first brought him to accept the Christianity for which he would now die. And he was joyous of that fact too, although the fear had returned to him now, trembling in his stomach and at his finger tips.

Every movement in the room made him start. He thought then the time had come, although through the window he could see the soldiers still at their parades, the marching, the music playing, the chanting of the crowds. And so the long hours passed by. Somewhere he knew in this Arena, the State President, would be sitting watching, in his embroidered, gilded, bemedalled clothes, rising to salute his soldiers as they passed, handing out awards to their commanders – a medal, a china horse, a gilded metal star set on a wooden stand.

Was that what soldiers vied for? He did not think so. So why did they fight? Not for some token reward, surely. For the danger? Yes, perhaps. And to be able to say you were a man, and had endured the worst that could ever be thrown at you? Yes, very likely too. Yet, he knew the real reason he had fought, and why he suffered now, was to find truth – truth in himself and, above all, the truth of God. To some this might sound insincere, pretentious, contemptible even. But to him it was the only thing in the world. And he would show his belief to be true by his own sacrifice.

The soldiers were leaving the Arena at last. The crowds still filled the part of the stands that Albanus could see from the window, and they were chanting now. Albanus could not make out what the chant said. The noise was growing louder. There seemed to be some disorder breaking out. An officer came into the room. He looked flustered. He spoke to the guard commander. Albanus overheard a few words. 'The President....been a change of plan....you'll be notified.' A great surge of hope filled Albanus's breast. Something in the programme had changed. Was he to be reprieved? Was his sacrifice not to be demanded after all?

He sat on looking out of the window. He was given a further sandwich. He could eat only a little of it. The crowds now seemed to be leaving the stands. The Arena floor had also emptied. Another officer came into the room and spoke in a whisper, which Albanus could not overhear. He was still told nothing. His bladder was full and he was escorted to relieve himself in a toilet nearby. His hands were released for the purpose, then immediately cuffed again.

When he returned, it was to find that everything had changed. He was told now of new arrangements. There was to be no reprieve. He was still going to die this day. But politics had made it necessary for the original plan to be altered.

The State President had been seated in the grand presidential box high in the Arena's northern stands when he was brought a written message by an emissary. It was an urgent communication, from the State's Foreign Affairs Department, which manned its old-fashioned electronic and digital communications systems twenty-four hours a day, national holiday or not. The message and its accompaniments spoke of a declaration made that morning by the World Council on Human Rights (the WCHR). The President knew of the power of the WCHR to interfere in the affairs of a nation – in his State too, just at the point when, after receiving some long-sought foreign investments, the State had begun to get its economy under control, and was gaining a higher esteem amongst its global partners.

The declaration stated. 'WCHR condemns use of capital sentences against popular opposition to policies of your State. It demands immediate cessation and review. Public execution not deemed acceptable by any nation seeking admission to WCHR or other global bodies. Confirm compliance with this demand at earliest opportunity, ensuring cases of all prisoners so affected are reviewed.'

Attached was another message, this one stamped 'The Holy See, Vatican City': 'Tolerance to all faith systems advised. Many advances made recently in Christian pragmatism provide adequate grounds for your desisting in persecution of traditional faith proselytes. A Plea for Mercy.'

The President grunted and muttered over the flimsy sheets of paper in his hand. Very well, he decided, the execution will not take place. Certainly, it will not take place here now, in full public view. We will declare we have granted the amnesty requested. But it *will be done*. It will be done elsewhere in secret. In time, my people will come to learn of this, if not the outside world, who will soon lose interest. The people will then know how I remain strong, and that I rule in accordance with our Party's policies. I will never give in to what the outside world tells me to do on matters so important to our State.

He spun around in his chair and issued a string of orders. Aides sprang into action.

When the crowd learnt the execution at the Arena had been cancelled, it expressed its displeasure vocally. Some seats were torn up in the stands, and cushions and other missiles thrown about. Arena stewards, armed with batons, soon had the situation under control, however, and the disappointed people began to file out through the Arena exits. But the rumour was already spreading that the execution was *not* in fact cancelled but only postponed: it would take place somewhere else. Once outside, beyond the Arena walls, many of the dispersing crowd saw and heard the army's vehicles parked in the entrance court re-starting their engines. Then they saw a figure led out, his head and torso covered by a black, plastic sheet thrown over his head, and they knew this must be the prisoner – Albanus, the traitor, sentenced to die today. Most did not know what his treasons had been, but they did not care. They wanted this Albanus's blood – to see it shed.

Some tried to stand in the way of the army lorry the prisoner had been thrown into, as it sought to get through the discontented crowd, with another truck full of soldiers following. People spilled around the revving vehicles. One man's legs were run over, and he was dragged away, screaming. Soldiers, brandishing heavy staves, dismounted from the truck, beating the crowd back, trying to clear a passage. Eventually they succeeded, and the army vehicles accelerated away. But some of the crowd were still following, yelling and cheering. Here was excitement. Here was action. Here was a hunt, a wild pursuit. The quarry was still in sight, held up now by a heavy lorry with a wide load of aircraft parts heading for the City's airport.

Only half a mile from the Arena was that same bridge crossing the river, where, in the meadow below, Albanus had been baptised. The two army vehicles carrying Albanus and his guards, escaping at last from the blockage that had delayed them, came up to the bridge, and then stopped before it, blocking the carriageway. The fastest-moving elements of the crowd, intent on the excitement of the chase, were close upon them. Soldiers hurriedly deployed across the bridge, their long staves swinging, preventing anyone going further.

Some of the pursuers, seeing the soldiers, poured down the road embankment into the meadow. Their intent – if they indeed had one in the mania now possessing them – seemed to be to get across the river along the line of the bridge piles, perhaps by swimming and scrambling. Finding this to be near impossible, those on the river edge stopped, casting their eyes up and down stream for an easier route, but there was none. Soon they were pressed from behind by others coming up. Many people – men in the main, but some women also, and even a child or two – were forced into the water. More came, more were pushed in. There grew a general pandemonium, a melee of shrieks and curses, people locked together, some thrusting back, some pushing forward, with those in the river out of their depth screaming and splashing hysterically, before sinking, a few rising, their flapping bodies floating away in the strong current out of sight, their shrieks stifled by the swirling waters. Meanwhile, the soldiers still lined the bridge, keeping back the ever growing crowds.

The lorry holding Albanus was now able to get away with no one in pursuit. Enveloped by the plastic cover which a guard held down over him, he had heard the yells of the crowd and sensed the lorry rocking and juddering, stopping, then starting again, the noise of its engine rising. The shouts of the guards beside him meant little to him. There was much coarse laughter. One guard shouted out, 'Let them drown.. Serves them f---ing right'. The lorry rumbled on relentlessly, picking up speed.

THE HILL

Execution

22

Where was he being taken? This journey, so unexpected, so broken by starts and stops, had shaken Albanus's equanimity. He had been ready for death in the Arena, but how would death be brought to him now? He knew that what was happening was but an alteration to the way he was to die. He called up his inner vision of the blessed Jesus Christ, how he too had been taken to his crucifixion in pain and torment. This vision, and the prayer he now offered up helped give him renewed strength to endure – 'Oh Lord, I offer up my life to you that my people shall know your goodness, even those who do this evil to me'.

He felt through the motion of the truck, its bumping and groaning, that they had left the tarred main road, and were on another, much rougher side road – but going where? What he couldn't see – bundled up like a parcel, handcuffed, half-stifled by the plastic sheet – was that they had entered land controlled by the army and used by them for training. There was a rifle range here, with a scatter of huts about it.

A hill rose from the river plain. It was not high, only a relatively low, rounded eminence, but it was prominent in the flat landscape. The crest of the hill was fringed by pine trees. There had been a derelict farmhouse below it, but the army had taken this over and demolished it, building their huts and stores in its place, and setting out a firing range with its row of targets against the hillside.

The truck came to a halt. Albanus felt its lurching movement stop as the engine was switched off. He was lifted out by his guards, and then pulled free of his covering. The light rushed at him like sudden fire and he blinked his eyes to absorb it. He saw the dull grey of the wooden-sided huts with their rusting metal roofs. One had a tall pipe for a chimney, with a cowl on its top. Two black ravens were perched on the roof ridge. They took off as he looked at them, and he followed them with his eyes, envying their freedom. He saw the hill now, its green, grassy slopes below a blue sky laced with trailing patches of white cloud, like sailing yachts upon a distant sea. He watched the ravens soaring high across the hill until they settled amongst the dark trees on the summit.

With his hands still bound before him, his guards close about him, he was led between the huts until he could see the firing points with their range targets beyond, set against the hill. Here, others were waiting for them: two army officers, in grey-green uniforms with flat caps and wearing high black boots, and some yards beyond them a tightly formed squad of soldiers in combat fatigues with rifles at their sides. Each soldier wore a black mask pulled up from his neck over his lower face.

Albanus's heart began pounding at the sight of them: he knew their purpose. He forced his gaze away and looked up at the hill, seeing the green slopes stirred by the breeze and the patches of yellow sunlight that sparkled there like pools of ever-moving waters. He tried to form a picture of the Holy Jesu. 'He leads me beside still waters. He restores my soul. He leads me in the paths of righteousness for His name's sake.' He felt a sudden sense of peace – a depth of peace he had scarcely ever experienced before. The way was right. There was nothing to fear. His mortal journey was almost over. This peace was but a tiny expression of the far greater peace that was to come.

As he was led forward by his guards, the harsh reality of the present returned to him. He was aware now of each tiny stone beneath his feet, each grass blade like a swinging scythe, each declivity in the ground a slope to be conquered. His legs seemed to be beyond his control, as if his mind was already half-detached from his body. How he longed to escape from it entirely. He yearned now for this last scene to be over.

He was stopped beside a large post set into the ground half-way along the length of the range; that the post had been placed there very recently was clear from the freshly upcast earth about it. The officers stood in front of him. To one side of them, he could see the soldiers of the firing party marching across his front, their rifles at the slope. They halted and ground arms. Behind them were the upper slopes of the hill with the silent pines along the crest and the vast blueness of the sky beyond.

An officer came face to face with him, a paper in his hand. Albanus could see his hands were shaking.

'Albanus Detrichen, it is my duty to carry out your execution for the crime of treason, as pronounced by the High Court of the State on 16th July last. Do you have any final request?'

'Yes, that I will not be bound in any way and have nothing over my eyes.' He was surprised at the steadiness of his voice, for now he could sense his whole body trembling and his heart racing.

'Very well.' The officer motioned to a guard behind him, who stepped forward and released Albanus's wrists from their cuffs. Then both men stepped back.

An order was shouted. The firing party in line took two paces forward and halted. Albanus held himself as upright as he could with the post at his back. A further order. The rifles came to the aim.

Albanus stared into them. He thought, I want to see everything. I want to see the very end, as at the beginning, the first worm that crawled out of the soil and became a man. I wish to die as a man. Oh world, how I have loved you. Forgive me my sins. My sweet Jesu.

'Fire!'

He felt a mighty blow, falling into a space of intense blackness – then, passing through into eternal light, he saw the face of God.

SYNCHRONICITY OF LIGHT

AD 305 – the present

23

The long grasses were alight with coloured flowers. How beautiful they were, he thought: reds, and blues, yellows and orange. Butterflies floated amongst them, lifted from bloom to bloom on a trickling breeze.

There were others with him on the hill. Turning his head, he could see a whole multitude from the town of Verulamium below him, some still crossing the river that flowed through the meadows beneath. They wore bright tunics and robes, and some bore branches of green leaf torn down from the trees, flourishing them in the sunlight.

Coming to the top of the hill, with his guards in their steel armour beside him, he saw that others were waiting there – more soldiers and a man in a white toga, which lay heavy upon him in the summer heat. A circlet of myrtle was about his brow and he held an ivory baton in his right hand. To one side of him, the executioner appeared, his sword already unsheathed, its blade glowing in the sun. He was dressed in a grey tunic with borders of red chevrons, and wore a mask of leather that hid much of his face, all but his mouth and eyes.

Albanus scanned the throng before him, and, yes, praise be, there was his aged father with tears running from his eyes, he in a tunic of dark wool. Beside him too, the two women he loved, weeping, with cloaks pulled tight about their bodies, despite the day's stilled heat.

And now they were pushing him forward, his head placed on a wooden block close to the busy earth, alive with all manner of crawling things. But he did not see these. He saw only the future and the world to be – the Cross and his dear Lord's face, and he knew this was glorious and not an ending at all.

The executioner raised the sword and the blade flashed down. Such was the energy of his stroke that his eyes popped out like stones and fell to the bloodied earth by Albanus's severed head.

At that moment, in this present age of our writing, the President of a distant country seated writing at his desk, felt a searing pain in his eyes. Trying to focus them on the white-painted wall before him, he saw only the black trunk of a tree dividing his vision, spreading ever wider. He called out for help, but no one came. He remembered then what that prisoner brought before him had told him:

'If you do not see the power of God when he is before you, you will not be able to see at all.'

And he was afraid then and screamed out in his agony.

As at the beginning, as at the ending, that scream never fades, never dies.

AFTERWORD

I first became interested in St. Alban, Britain's protomartyr, after visiting the cathedral at St. Albans many years back and watching Professor Martin Biddle's excavations ahead of the construction of a new Chapter House. I learnt of the professor's ambition to locate the first martyrium church of the saint, unfortunately not realised, although an alternative site alongside the known Roman cemetery to the south of the Cathedral, I understand, remains a possibility. The story from Bede, and other early sources, of the flowery hill that St. Alban climbed to his execution, and the manner of his martyrdom, made a lasting impression on me.

I believe it is possible to look at the story of St. Alban in contexts and time frames other than the historically-attested 3rd or early 4th century AD. Thus, I have set my re-imagining of these events in the present day, or perhaps the very near future.

A particular puzzle to me was why the priest, Amphibalus, allowed Alban to take his place and go to martyrdom rather than doing so himself. I present a possible interpretation. We are told Amphibalus continued to preach and baptise, but was to receive his own martyrdom later. His shrine, recently reconstructed, is close to that of St. Alban in the cathedral.

This book is dedicated to a friend. It was a late November day over thirty years ago when we came to St. Albans. The trees on the hill were losing their last leaves, which were spiralling down, lit by wondrous shafts of pale yellow sunlight. We looked at an exhibition in the cathedral where I read of how and why St. Alban died. I told her that one day I would write this book.

And now it is done.

William Foot (writing as John Aubin)
November 2024